＄ ＄ ＄

"Are you trying to seduce me?" she whispers.

"I think so." I kiss her again. "Why don't we move to the back seat?"

She steps out of the car; I crawl over the seat. We face each other, not talking, just staring. She pulls off her shirt, never once removing her gaze from me. She grabs my arms and pulls me on top of her. I graze my lips along her jawline and whisper, "I don't actually believe this is happening."

She moans, holds me tight, and roughly kisses my neck. "How does this feel?" she asks.

"Wonderful."

We roll over. Her hair falls across my face and chest; its softness makes me shudder. She yanks my jeans down to my hips, then wraps herself around me. I feel I am floating high above all those twinkling lights, high above the smog. We swirl together over the city until all the separate lights become one.

Her hands and lips and fingers touch every part of me, until I cry out. I have wanted this so much. We speed down toward earth, and I manage to breathe out "Wow."

She lays the back of her hand softly on my cheek. "Mmm. That was nice. It's been awhile."

"It was incredible. You're incredible. I can't believe... God, I love you. I totally love you. I'd do anything for you."

Silence. Dead silence.

It dawns on me that I may have made a terrible mistake.

＄ ＄ ＄

SIDE

DISH

KIM TAYLOR

RISING
TIDE
PRESS

Rising Tide Publishers
65161 Emerald Ridge Dr.
Tucson, AZ 85739
520-888-1140

Printed in the United States on acid-free paper.

Publisher's note:
All characters, places and situations in this book are fictitious, and any resemblance to persons (living or dead) is purely coincidental.

Publisher's acknowledgments:
Special thanks to Edna G. for believing in us, and to the feminist and gay bookstores for being there.

First printing December, 1998
10 9 8 7 6 5 4 3 2 1

Edited by Sonya Cashdan
Cover Art by Sally Rogers, Red Horse Graphics, Inc.

Side Dish/Kim Taylor
p.cm
ISBN   1-883061-18-0

Library of Congress Catalog Card Number 98-73137

DEDICATION

For J. S. H.

ACKNOWLEDGMENTS

I wish to thank my editor, Sonya Cashdan, and Rising Tide Press for their support of this book. Thanks also to Leslie, Pam, Timmie and Steve, and Kim for their early encouragement and enthusiasm. Most of all, I want to thank Jennifer for her guidance, advice, editorial excellence, and for being the altogether most special one.

CHAPTER 1

I get in my Saab to go to work at Mexicali Joe's (home of the best margarita in Los Angeles) on one of those mornings when the brown-yellow smog of a million cars has already strangled any available bit of sunlight. I have yet to get up at 5 a.m. to breathe the ten minutes of clean air, but, hey, it could happen.

I pull the car onto La Brea, pissed off at the ugliness of the closed-up, one-story, fake-adobe monstrosities that pass as architecture in this part of town. It's always an adventure driving these city streets, hangover or not. Drivers cut in front of you, turning right with their left turn signals on; a couple of homeless people decide to cross when your light is green; and you always have to watch out for cop cars surrounding yet another drug bust which blocks your lane.

Okay, so this morning I get it all: cops, jaywalkers, cutters. This day is not starting out well. Add the fact that I didn't get to sleep until 4 a.m., because someone didn't turn off their car alarm. And now, I'm late, which means I'll have to wipe down and set up every table. See, if you're early, you get the cushy job of refilling the salt and pepper and spooning sour cream into little bowls.

Well, with good tips and super strong margaritas, who can complain?

Now, I'm not a has-been actress who hasn't had a gig in a while. I'm not Daddy's Little Girl, taking time out from the country club to see what adventures await in the big bad world. I'm just a waitress. I bought my Saab down in Long Beach for $500. It's got a gray primer finish, a rag as a gas cap, and no back seat . . . but it's mine. And I don't have to worry about anyone stealing it, you know?

I'm twenty-six years old with a bachelor's degree in the not-so-highly employable field of anthropology. I moved to L.A. because I didn't have any better ideas. I've been here three years, worked as a clerk in an overpriced salon, been a commercial agent's assistant, and labored one long day in B. Dalton's. I've been at Mexicali Joe's for eleven months, the longest I've held a job. Ever. I'd move on, but I wouldn't know where to go.

So here I am wiping down tables in the main dining room, basking in the silence before the mariachi tape breaks my eardrums. The room is actually a patio, with a canvas roof that can be rolled back to let in the sunlight and exhaust fumes. It's already 80 degrees, so I assume the busboys will open the lid. This creates a lovely dining experience for the customers, and allows me to get a sunburn and sweat marks under my armpits. By noon, I'll look like the waitress from hell. I can't wait to have a Kamikaze.

Jeff's humming to himself up by the bar, filling the salt shakers as if he were pouring holy water into crystal vials. From the back, he's one of those unbelievably good-looking guys: perfect muscles, tight butt, wavy brown hair. He could model for Guess, if his face didn't look so much like Himmler's.

Oh, he's not like Himmler, trust me. He's my best friend. We do a lot together, much to the annoyance of his boyfriend, Mark, a macrobiotic/gym junkie who doesn't enjoy going bar hopping or staying up late listening to Irene Kral. He'll call my apartment in the wee hours of the morning, asking for Jeff. Jeff and I don't have to worry about the time, because we know Mark will call to let us know when our evening is over.

As I scratch dried salsa off a plastic tablecloth, I call out to Jeff, "Hey, wanna go to the Rifle tonight?"

"Sorry. I'm going to the gym with Mark at seven o'clock."

"It's two-for-one beer night. I could pick you up at nine."

"Well, since you put it that way . . . sure."

We go back to our respective tasks. For some reason, I've been thinking about the word "waitress." The manager told me that he prefers the word "server." I don't know; I feel "waitress" is more to the point. Sort of like "stewardess" or "seamstress" or "governess." That "e-s-s" says it all—Female Slave. Perhaps we could use the word "waitron": gender-free and entirely robotic.

"Hey, Mutt, it's Monday. You-Know-Who is coming in."

Jeff calls me Mutt. I know. Mutt 'n' Jeff. It's been my nickname ever since I started here. I tell people to knock it off, but the name seems to have stuck. I mean, who the hell are Mutt 'n' Jeff, anyway?

I hate when he teases me about "You-Know-Who." It's just a woman I have a crush on and wouldn't dare talk to, besides saying, "What can I get you?" After all, I'm Mutt, and she's a dead ringer for Judy Davis. She has these piercing hazel eyes and an intelligently moody expression. She's practically perfect. I mean, the only thing I see wrong is her nose. It's a little crooked, that's all, and from certain angles (believe me, I've checked them all) it looks like someone popped her one as a kid.

I have a love/hate relationship with her: I love her in my dreams, but face to face, she reminds me of my lower-than-snot status in life. Not that she'd know the suffering my self-esteem goes through. She barely looks my way.

Juan, the busboy, breaks rudely into my reverie. He taps my shoulder and points to Table 12. He doesn't say anything, just continues on his way to the chip drawer. Juan's not a very talkative guy. Actually, I've never heard him say a word. Or seen him crack a smile. Apparently, his wife and two little girls still live in Mexico, and he hasn't seen them in three years. He supposedly sends all his money back to them and lives with four other brothers in a studio apartment near Sunset and Western. He's never told the tale himself. It sounds like a million other immigrant stories, so it may or may not be true. But the story's true for someone out there in this city, that's for sure.

I grab my pad and assume a slavish smile as I approach Table 12. It's a good tip group: four very well-dressed gay men. They're the best—they run a high bill, buy you a drink, and leave a 25% tip, on average. This group comes in every Monday from their interior design firm around the corner. They order the easiest items on the menu: a pitcher of margaritas (no salt) and two full orders of fajitas. Cool. Easy. If I can get everyone to order like this, my day will be a piece of cake.

I take care of their order in five minutes flat, which leaves me enough time to go smoke a cigarette out back. Jeff can take the next table.

I smoke out by the valet parking lot; it's pretty private, because the valets ignore the restaurant staff. I'm on the third drag of my Marlboro Light, enjoying the sun, when "You-Know-Who's" Mercedes glides into the lot. Shit.

Okay, stub out the cig, take a deep breath, and relax. I go into the bathroom to wash my hands and shoot some breath spray in my mouth. I'm ready. Out I go, hoping she's sitting in Jeff's section so I can gaze discreetly from afar. My self-esteem's playing its little game: I'm fat, my pants are too tight, I have a shitty hair cut and blotchy skin. I break out in a clammy sweat.

She sits at a window table facing the garden, with two friends I've never seen before.

In my section.

It's only 11 a.m.

I was up until four.

"Hi, what can I get you?" I say, oh-so-gracefully.

Judy (I don't know her real name) glances up and gives me one of those ambiguous half-smiles generally reserved for idiots and little kids. Unlike me, she's not fat, wears Ann Taylor clothing like a dream, and her perm cost her at least $175. I could die right here. I look at her two friends, dressed in Rodeo Drive slouch, looking homeless for probably, oh, a mere $500. Obviously writers or actors of some sort, they probably don't have to work more than two weeks a year for a living.

I'm not exaggerating. I know a girl who is a spokesman for a certain steak sauce company (which will remain nameless). Once a year, for three days, she shoots three commercials that will air throughout our great land. She makes $57,000. I kid you not.

You remember the scene in *L.A. Story* where everyone orders double decaf cappuccinos with a twist? Check this out:

FRIEND #1: Do you have any vegetarian items?

ME: We can take the meat off any item.

FRIEND #2: What does that mean?

ME: There won't be any meat on anything. (Duh.)

FRIEND #2: You mean, anything on the menu?

ME: Well, it's a little hard to take the chicken out of chicken mole.

FRIEND #2: Are your refried beans vegetarian?

ME: Of course. (I'm lying.)

(They bury their heads in their menus, ignoring me entirely. After an eternity punctuated by sweat dripping down my sides, JUDY DAVIS raises her head.)

JUDY: Um . . . (She turns to FRIEND #1) You first.

FRIEND #1: I'd like two beef soft tacos with no beef, no cheese, and a dollop of sour cream. On the side.

JUDY: That sounds fine. I'll have the same.

ME: So you basically want tortillas and shredded lettuce, right?

(They look at me blankly.)

ME: Never mind.

(I turn to FRIEND #2.)

ME: Would you like the same?

FRIEND #2: No, I'll have the carnitas.

ME: You do realize that's PORK?!

FRIEND #2: Yeah, whatever. That comes with refried beans, right?

ME: You mean, the vegetarian refried beans?

FRIEND #2: Okay. That's fine.

JUDY: Do you have decaffeinated iced tea?

ME: Of course. (I lie again.)

JUDY: I'll have a margarita on the rocks. No salt.

FRIEND #1: I'll have the same. But nonalcoholic.

FRIEND #2: I'll have the same—no, make it a shot of tequila.

ME: Have you guys seen *L.A. Story?*

(They look at me blankly.)

ME: Never mind.

If these are her friends, I may have to question my crush judgment.

I end up having to work a double, as Denise calls to say she can't make it. I don't know what it is with these waitrons. They feel they can come and go as they please, with no thought that someone like me will have to stay and miss my evening at the Rifle. When I get home to my squalid apartment (and that's an optimistic description) I smell like a plate of burnt fajitas and my shirt drips with guacamole and oil. Well, at least I made enough in tips to cover my ten-days-overdue car insurance.

I pop open a beer and turn on David Letterman. He's interviewing some hot-shit new actress who thinks corn rows make her attractive to the opposite sex. I'm mesmerized by the eerie whiteness of her scalp. It's reflecting all the studio lights and sending out beams of pink and green. As she turns her head toward Dave, the light from her scalp hits him smack in the eyes, and for one second I think he's suffered major retinal damage. I hope when she watches the tape tomorrow, she'll scream all the way to her Beverly Hills hairdresser.

I light a cig and down another beer. I hate this time of night, when I'm too tired to go out and too restless to sit. I look out the window, which has a view of a gravel roof. It's about 425 degrees in here, so I make an attempt to pry open the window. No luck; it's painted shut. I search my desk drawer for a screwdriver and hammer. I'm about to slam the screwdriver into the window paint, but I realize I'll probably wake up everyone on the block. I drop the tools on the floor as a reminder to try again in the morning. Yeah, right. I live in a hermetically sealed oven; a nuclear blast wouldn't open this window.

God, what I would give for a different life. And a window that opens.

CHAPTER 2

It's about 10 a.m. on my day off. Jeff and I sit on the floor of his apartment, listening to *Gertrude Stein, Gertrude Stein, Gertrude Stein* on the record player. It's one of our favorite things to do, and we trade off saying the lines along with the actress playing ol' Gert.

We're drinking really strong coffee out of authentic French mugs. You know the kind of cup: it takes two hands and a forklift to hold. We're on our second gallon, so the caffeine is just beginning to kick in. We splurge, eating baguettes with brie, and smoking Marlboro Reds.

"Maybe if I smoke enough of these, I can sound like Suzanne Pleshette," I say.

"Why would you want to sound like her?"

"I've always had a thing for Emily on the *Bob Newhart Show.*

Jeff laughs and lights another cigarette. I resent the way he smokes. He's sexy and suave, and knows how to blow smoke as if he were kissing someone. I just smoke like a smoker. Inhale, burn the lungs, exhale.

"Jeff, don't you wish we were expatriates in Paris? We could be sitting in a cafe in Montmartre listening to the real Gertrude Stein."

"Yeah, that would have been a great life. I could dig myself in a black beret."

"Or lounging in white linen on the Mediterranean."

"With a soft breeze caressing our skin."

"Yeah," I sigh.

Jeff sighs, too, and we sink into our separate dreams.

"Where's Mark?" I ask. Usually Mark lurks around in their bedroom, doing God knows what, until Jeff and I have finished our Parisian mornings. I don't think Mark likes me very much.

"He's at acting class, then he's starting a job as a bartender."

"You're kidding! He doesn't even drink."

"He needs money to pay for more acting classes."

"Where's he working?"

"The Butthole. It's off Santa Monica Boulevard."

"The Butthole?! You're joking. The Butthole? That's unbelievable; who'd name a bar something like that? Yeah, let's go to the Butthole for a beer, and then to the Penis for dinner!"

Jeff throws up his hands and retorts, "Hey, it's West Hollywood."

"Is it a guy thing?" I ask, thoroughly puzzled.

"It's very trendy."

I pop a piece of baguette in my mouth, shake my head, and say, "It's very weird."

Jeff turns the record over and Gertrude Stein begins Act Two.

❖   ❖   ❖

I'm wandering along Melrose Avenue, looking at the millions of things not to buy, and wondering what to do with the rest of my day off. I grab an *LA Weekly* and check out the movies. I scan the entries for anything that isn't a slasher techno-thriller, when my eye catches on an ad for *The Brady Bunch Movie* currently playing at a revival house nearby. I love the Brady Bunch. I can't help it. Those guys are normal, boring, and utterly immortal. It gives me hope that, one of these days, someone will make a Partridge Family movie.

Back in junior high, I wanted to look like Keith Partridge. I would dress in a dark blue polyester shirt and tight white pants, comb my hair so it had that cool center part, lock the door to the bathroom, and sing in front of the mirror. I was partial to the songs "I Think I Love You" and "I Can Feel Your Heart Beat." When I look at pictures of myself from that time, I am dismayed by the fact that I really resembled Danny. When you've got freckles and red hair, the "Keith Look" is completely unreachable.

Now, I don't want to give the impression that I'm a total loser. I also love esoteric Russian films and anything by Woody Allen. Hey, *The Last Metro* is my favorite movie, so I do have some taste. I also pride myself on being well-read. By the time I was fourteen I had read all of Jane Austen and Charles Dickens. I devoured Virginia Woolf's novels in a month, and I adore Jeanette Winterson. I've read the Romantic poets and Paris writers of the twenties. I did all this before and after college. In school, we only read the dead white male authors. Boring.

I'll make a confession. I also read trashy girl books. At least one a week. I dig the girl-meets-girl-and-has-to-leave-her-(possibly murderous)-husband plotlines. I love Beebo Brinker, with her dated, but definitely hip, attire. And if I could fly to Australia and marry Inspector Carol Ashton, I would. But I wouldn't tell anybody I read these books, any more than I'll cop to the fact that I'm going to *The Brady Bunch Movie* again. It's a matter of personal pride.

As I leave the movie, I'm still laughing over the girl who's in love with Marcia. Frankly, I never got into Marcia. She reminds me of my older sister, Sandra, reigning queen of Modesto high society. I feel Jan is the most interesting of the Brady girls. I connect with her second-best soul.

CHAPTER 3

She whispers, "Come here."

"Why?" I ask.

"I want to kiss you."

My stomach does a 360 and lands with a thud. I can't breathe.

"Come here," she demands, a smile playing the corners of her lips.

I slowly pick up my feet, both of them heavy as tugboats, and approach her. She places her hand behind my neck and pulls me towards her.

It's some kiss. Her lips are soft and greedy. All of my concentration surrounds this kiss; it's heart-stoppingly incredible. Lips and tongue and breath and snapping fingers.

She's snapping her fingers. I don't get it. She keeps snapping as I melt into her.

"Mutt. Oh, Mutt!"

My name sounds like spring rain coming from her mouth.

"Mutt. Hello!"

"Huh?"

"Get a grip. You have food sitting on the counter."

"What?" I stammer.

"Mutt, pick up your food. It's getting cold."

What is Jeff doing here? Where's Judy Davis? Slowly, the tables come into focus, and the humming noise of the customers bombards my ears. I shake my head, forcing these intrusions to disappear. They don't. I'm here. Damn.

I pick up my food order, dodging angry looks from the kitchen staff. I don't say I'm sorry. They don't deserve it. One of them stole my bike the first week I was here. I found it hidden around the side of the building. If I were Lauren Laurano, I would have nabbed the thief in the space of a week. But I'm not, so I haven't.

I turn around from serving the semi-warm food and see two old friends walk in. Well, not friends, exactly, but two girls I used to party with, Deb and Sue. They run a florist shop in the Valley. They haven't been in the restaurant for months. They see me and wave. Sue has big, brown eyes and messy hair. Deb looks like she's gained weight. Deb looks like she's pregnant.

I hug them and realize Deb actually *is* pregnant. Whoa.

After they sit, Sue starts rubbing Deb's back, while I pick my jaw up off the floor.

"You . . . you're . . . you're pregnant," I stammer.

"Yeah, can you believe it?" Sue replies ecstatically.

"Was it planned?" Why do I always sound like such an idiot? Two gay women can't exactly have a *little accident.*

Luckily, Deb ignores my stupidity and explains, "Well, no, it wasn't."

"I'm not following."

"Deb went on a camping trip with three guys. Up in Tahoe."

"I went to college with them," Deb interjects. She moves her hand gently back and forth over her stomach.

"Anyway," Sue continues, "she slept with one of them, a guy she used to date in college."

I look from one to the other in complete astonishment.

"What was I supposed to do?" Sue says. "Break up with her now that she's going to have a baby? I don't think so."

"Yeah, yeah. Right. Sure. Whatever. Um, what can I get you?"

I'm dumbfounded. I mean, really, your girlfriend sleeps with an old boyfriend, gets knocked up, and runs back to you? Personally, I'd have thrown Deb's things in the middle of Van Nuys Boulevard and moved to Alaska.

When I think of it, the old Sue would have done that. And worse. I spent many a late night watching them have jealous catfights when one or the other flirted with whoever was in the nearest bar seat. I vaguely remember a really late night when Sue and I moved Deb's couch, coffee table, plates, and omelet pan out of their house and onto the lawn. Deb then ripped the hell out of Sue's clothes.

I don't know these two blissfully happy people. I retreat into my waitron mode and hope the aliens will leave soon.

A baby! I can't even keep a pet. I had a cat once in college, but we didn't have very good chemistry. If I sat on the couch, she would slink along the back and pounce on my ear. I had so many scratches on my earlobes, you would have thought I was into some weird masochistic cult that believed the ear was the source of all evil. Once, the cat cornered me. She glowered in the doorway; I cowered on the bed. I had no escape. That cat wanted to take me down. We stared warily at each other for two hours, until I gave up and fell asleep.

I called that cat Destiny. Buying her was my first mistake. My second mistake? I tried desperately to love her. Hey, I was lonely. I thought we'd be a little family. I would pick her up, cuddle her, coo in her ear. One day, she slashed my cheek open. Then she used my breast as a diving board. Blood streamed copiously from my right cheek and left breast. Destiny then proceeded to hurl herself out of my screenless window. I lived on the second story. I couldn't bear to look at the inevitable cat splat on the driveway below.

A minute later, Destiny, whom I had assumed to be dead, slunk into the room. She hissed at me, meandered into the bedroom, ensconced herself on my pillow, and began to lick her butt.

Fearing that she had come back to wreak the vengeance of the undead, I gave her to an unsuspecting professor the next day. I watched in despair as that miserable furball curled in the prof's lap and began to purr.

A baby? No way. I'd be too afraid.

CHAPTER 4

The Rifle, an extremely popular club, has a huge dance floor, a great sound system, and a separate back room for the girls. Jeff and I sit in the guys' section; the girls' area is, typically, allotted half the space and is shoved in the back of the building. This room is called the Femme Room, while the girls' is named the Butch Room. How cleverly original.

We lucked out earlier and got a curved booth all to ourselves. It has a great view of the cavernous dance floor, where guys bump and grind, and sweat glistens on every chest. The women dance near the sidelines. There are only a few of them, also grinding away, but to a much slower beat than the music actually playing.

Jeff has just come back from the bar, having successfully negotiated the teeming room while hanging on to two shots of tequila and two longnecks.

"There's a table open in the back," he informs me. "Why don't we sit in there?"

"What?"

Jeff yells in my ear, "Let's sit in the back; it's quieter!"

I shake my head and pat the booth as a signal for him to stay put.

"It's too loud out here!" he screams.

"No, it's not!" I shout back.

"Come on." He picks up his beer and shot, and motions with his head for me to follow.

I guess I have no choice, but I really don't want to go in the back room. I have a hard time being around so many women, and have been known to break out in hives when surrounded by them.

As we walk through the doorway, I notice the decibel level drops to about one-quarter of that out front. The long bar, with booths and smoked mirrors along the facing wall, looks very deco, done in black, mauve, and white. A large TV plays a Melissa Etheridge video. Women sit in couples or small groups, heads together, joined in secret conversations. No one looks up when Jeff and I come in; at least, I think they don't. I'm looking at my feet. I feel my face go beet red, and blood pounds painfully in my temples.

We sit at a small booth. I stretch my arm along the top of the booth and slowly cross my legs, trying to pull off the nonchalant look. I hope it's working.

"Okay, much better," Jeff says.

"We could have stayed out front."

"What's wrong?"

"What?"

"You're ripping your napkin into shreds."

I look down. He's right. I have thoroughly shredded my napkin in the space of thirty seconds. I wad it up and stuff it in the pocket of my jeans. I belt back my tequila and take a swig of beer.

"Mutt, that woman's checking you out."

"No way. Where?"

"At the corner of the bar. The blonde."

I look sideways in the darkened mirror and pretend to fix my bangs. I see her: long, curly blonde hair, a button nose, and—oh shit. She knows I'm looking at her. She stares at my reflection and gives me a slow, lopsided grin. She has straight white teeth and dimples. I pretend to ignore her and turn my gaze toward Jeff.

"She probably recognizes me from the restaurant."

"Go talk to her."

"No."

"Go on!"

"No, Jeff. God, what would I say? I'd sound stupid. I don't even know her."

"That's why you introduce yourself."

"Whatever. I'm not into blondes, anyway."

"Well, I'm going to get us more cigarettes."

I grab Jeff's sleeve as he stands up.

"Jeff! Jeff, I'll get the cigarettes."

"Would you mellow out, Mutt?"

I clutch his hand in a death grip.

"Don't do this to me, Jeff. Please don't leave me here alone."

I'm ready to drop to my knees and plead for my life. Jeff removes my hand and sighs. "I'll be right back."

He'll be right back. I'm stuck at a table in a room full of women. My chest burns. I look in the mirror and breathe a sigh of relief when I see the blonde is gone. I close my eyes, try to gather my wits, but I feel like I'm on a Tilt-o-Whirl. The tequila has certainly done its job. I breathe out slowly to steady myself.

"Hi."

I open my eyes to Curly and her crooked grin sitting across from me.

"Hi," I say, because I'm so on the ball.

"Do I know you?"

I'd give up my firstborn child for Jeff to get back right now.

Curly crosses her arms on the table and looks right into my eyes. Wow, are her eyes blue or what?

"I *do* know you. We went to San Jose State together. The 'Deconstructing Athena' seminar?"

"Really?"

"Yeah. I knew you looked familiar. I'm Diane."

She shakes my hand with a grip that borders on abuse.

"Firm handshake," I say.

"Thanks."

She keeps staring at me with that goofy smile. I feel pinned to my seat by her cosmetically faultless teeth.

"Um, would you like a beer?" I ask.

"Actually, I have one at the bar. I'll go get it."

Diane jumps up and skips over to the bar. She whispers something to her friends, looking over her shoulder to wink at me. I swear, she actually winks. I give her a half-assed smile and furtively look around for Jeff. The jerk. He's probably out front dancing with one of the three hundred people he knows here.

Diane plops back down in what should be Jeff's seat.

"Here," she says, "I bought you a beer. I was in Women's Studies."

"Really? That was supposed to be a terrific program." Not Women's Studies. Let's join hands and sing "Kumbayah." She probably works at the Bookstore of the Seven Sisters and doesn't shave her armpits. Great.

"You were in English, right?" she asks.

"Yep. I mean, no. I was in anthropology."

"Really? My best friend is an anthropologist."

"Oh."

I'm not in the mood for reliving my college days with someone whose thesis most likely referenced *WomynSpeak* and *Sappho Lives!*. I'm not in the mood to relive my college days with anyone. I spent college trying to hang on to any thread of reality I could find, and Women's Studies majors stayed way out in LaLa Land.

"So," she chirps.

"So," I mimic.

"What are you doing now?"

"Um, I'm sitting here talking to you?"

"No," she laughs, "I mean in life."

"I'm studying nuclear physics at Cal Tech."

"Really?" Diane asks, looking stunned and impressed.

I can't lie. "Nah. I actually wait tables at Mexicali Joe's."

"Oh. I've been there a few times for dinner. I've never seen you there."

"I work days. I'm not ready for the night shift. I keep failing the customer relations test."

"Are you kidding?"

"I'm kidding. So, what about you?" I really need to scratch my chest.

"Me?"

"No, your imaginary friend sitting to your left." I smile as I say this, so I don't come off too snotty.

"I teach freshman comp at Pasadena City College."

"Wow, that's great."

"Yeah, it leaves me time to write."

"What are you writing?" I ask. Please don't say a screenplay. Everybody and their mother writes screenplays in this town.

"A book of poetry. I'm having a reading at Out and About Books next Wednesday. Why don't you come?"

"Well, I—"

"Look, I've got to get back to my friends. Here's my card. Call sometime."

"Okay."

"It was nice running into you." She turns toward her friends, hesitates, then says, "I'm sorry, but I don't remember your name."

"Mutt."

"Excuse me?"

"People call me Mutt. It's a nickname."

"Mmm. You're too cute to be called Mutt. See ya."

I smile and give her a little wave. She rejoins her friends, and they leave through a side door.

"Well?" Jeff asks, appearing out of nowhere.

"Where the hell did you go?"

"Dancing. Giving you space."

"Thanks a lot."

"What? Did she ask you out?"

"No. She remembered me from college. She's giving a poetry reading at Out and About next week."

"Did she ask you to go?"

"Sort of."

"Good. Very, very good."

"Let's just go back to my place and play quarters."

We wind our way through the sardine can of sexuality, and once outside, the fresh air sobers me up immediately. We hurry to the liquor store before it closes.

I sit in the car while Jeff's getting the beer, and look down my shirt to examine the hives. Wow. Just one. I'm impressed with myself.

As we drive back to my cell, I say to Jeff, "Maybe I should go to Diane's reading. After all, it's my birthday next

Wednesday and I need to celebrate in some way. Besides, you're working."

"Why don't we hit the drag shows in the Valley next Saturday?"

"Nah, it's kind of a downer to celebrate after the fact." I roll down the window and let the wind whip through my hair. "You know, Jeff, I just might do it."

"What?"

"Go to the reading. I mean, she said I was cute; that's got to count for something, right?"

CHAPTER 5

My sister called this morning from LAX to wish me happy birthday. She couldn't stop by, because she was on her way to a pharmacists' convention in Phoenix. She apologized about twenty times. I don't know why she bothers. I haven't seen her since she unloaded me at college, and I only hear from her when she's passing through the airport. She's too cheap to call from her prefab barf-pink house in the northern California 'burbs.

The big 2-7. Any way you look at it, it's bad. I'm too old to be doing what I'm doing. I used to think I'd be the next Richard Leakey. I'd jaunt about on fabulous digs: carefree, independent, and extremely popular with the cultural elite. At least, the girls of the cultural elite. Maybe it's my age, but I have a feeling that independence is more lonely than people let on.

Today, I'm buying myself a pair of cowboy boots with money I've saved just for this occasion. I walk into a tiny discount boot store on the Sunset Strip, and my eyes scout out the perfect pair: black, pointed toe, walking heel. Clean and mean. I slip them on, sighing at the comfort. Who wants tennis shoes when you can have Tony Lamas? I lay down the money and have enough left over for two pairs of boot socks.

I stride into Mexicali Joe's like I own it. I'm here to have my birthday lunch, 1/2 off. I don't work Wednesdays, so I won't run into any regular customers. I sit at a table in the corner so I'm not conspicuous. I hate public celebrations: birthdays, Christmas, 4th of July, you name it. They are just too stupid.

To my great relief, no one bothers me while I chomp on my chimichanga in peaceful solitude. Even Jeff leaves me alone, because the restaurant is packed. I'm getting ready to leave when the manager brings over a flan with a candle stuck in it. Jeff and Stephen, the other day waiter, come over and sing "Happy Birthday" in raucous voices. I'm mortified. And to top off this embarrassingly public moment, everyone in the restaurant applauds. They don't know me at all, but applaud anyway. Lemmings.

I get out of there as fast as I can. I've got a few hours to kill until the poetry reading at seven, so I ease the Saab onto Laurel Canyon and cut off at Mulholland for a scenic drive. If I look straight up, the sky is actually blue. If I look to the north, however, I get a good view of smog where the Valley should be. The only things visible in the dirty air are the scrawny ash-green tops of the palm trees that punctuate southern California like acne.

My temperature gauge hangs in the red, so I slow to a 20 m.p.h. crawl. You gotta take care with these foreign cars. I shift down to second around a tight curve; then, as I start to shift up, my clutch slips. I'm stuck in second gear. I floor it and try again, only to watch all the lights flash on my dash as the car dies. I coast down a steep hill, looking for a turnoff, and aim the car at a small clearing overhung with oaks. As the car rolls off the street, I hear a branch scrape paint off my roof. I turn the key. An asthmatic cough, then silence, greet me.

I get out and kick the door shut. I'm stuck somewhere between Bel Air and Brentwood amidst mansions guarded by dogs, cameras, and spy planes. In other words, there's not a human being in sight. Pissed off, I kick the car again, and my boot gets stuck on the metal bumper. Oh, great, I've ripped the side of my four-hour-old Tony Lamas boot.

I have no choice but to walk to Laurel Canyon and catch a bus back to civilization. It's not more than four or five miles. I think. I grab my backpack and baseball cap from the piece-of-shit car and trudge away.

This walk's not so bad. I've walked for thirty minutes, and actually enjoy the nature and quiet.

At the hour mark, these boots aren't so comfortable anymore. I can feel blisters popping on my heels and little toes. Guess I was wrong about the boots. And the distance.

Smog and dirt compact on my face. I feel like crying. Finally, I see a light on the horizon. Glinting proudly in the sun stands the bus sign. I stagger to the pole, so happy to have reached it that I don't mind waiting for the bus.

Forty-five minutes later, I hop on the Savior Express and reach in my pocket for change. I pull out thirty-five cents and drop it in the coin slot.

The bus driver stares at me, waiting for something. I move to sit down, and he says, "Bus fare is $1.10."

"Oh, okay."

I check my front and back pockets; I dig deep in my backpack.

"Um, I don't have enough money. My car broke down on Mulholland, and I've walked all the way here. Could I pay the rest later?"

The driver looks at me impassively. He's seen shirkers like me before, and he's having none of it.

"Full fare or no ride."

"You're kidding," I say. "I'll write a check, I'll—"

"Pay or walk."

Tears start to carve rivulets through the grunge on my cheeks. "Please, it's my birthday."

"Ma'am, please exit the bus."

I hear hostile murmurs coming from the back.

"Ma'am, exit the bus."

"I'll pay for her. For goodness' sake, what is this world coming to?"

A hunched-up old woman shakes her head as she slowly gets up from her seat to pay my fare.

"Thank you," I say as I sit down. I sniffle once. "You have no idea what this means to me."

"We would have sat here for hours, otherwise."

She turns away and stares out the front window as the bus winds its way down the canyon. I hope she knows that, by L.A. standards, her deed has put her in the realm of angels.

❖   ❖   ❖

I lurk across the street from Out and About, watching all the women go in to hear the poetry reading. I cleaned myself up after the Saab fiasco, determined at all costs to follow through on this commitment I've made to myself. However, I've got to keep a close eye on the woman/hive dilemma.

Okay, get it together. Diane may be happy I'm coming to her reading. I check my ponytail to make sure no hair has fallen out and boldly jaywalk across the street.

There's a picture of Diane in the window. She's kind of cute, in a perky way. The women inside the store look well-dressed and smart. I had better sit in the back, so my mongrel attire doesn't offend the intellectuals.

Oh, Jesus. I can't believe it. I can't go in. Judy You-Know-Who Davis is there. No way. I didn't have time to wash the gunk out of my hair before catching the bus here, which is why I have a ponytail. I can't deal with her shiny auburn tresses.

I turn quickly toward the Rifle. I'll have a beer and head home on the eight o'clock bus. Any later, I'd run the risk of being the only sane rider aboard.

"Hey, hey, wait a minute!"

I look in a store window so, out of the corner of my eye, I can see who's yelling. It's Diane. For a second, I think she's calling to me, but I can't be sure. I pretend not to hear and walk on.

"Mutt! Come back!"

I continue to walk, ignoring her completely. I'm just not up for that kind of crowd tonight. Especially not Judy Davis. And poetry seems so trivial when you're without a safe means of transportation. Besides, I have a two-inch rip in my new boot; I've had about all the blows my ego can handle.

I walk into the Rifle, order a beer at the front bar, and zone out on videos. It's 6:58 p.m. Twenty-seven years ago to the minute, I made my ill-fated appearance in this world. Happy fucking birthday, Mutt.

CHAPTER 6

I get on my bike to go to work at Mexicali Joe's because—surprise—my car was stolen up on Mulholland last night. The only thing left was gray primer along the underside of an oak branch. I don't know how the thieves got the Saab started again. If they didn't suffer such an aversion to nine-to-five jobs, they could make a killing as mechanics.

Why do bad things happen to so-so people? I mind my own business, just trying to have a good time, but God decides to play a little joke on me. He must be starved for stand-ups in heaven.

Every customer at the restaurant today has complained about something not being right; I can't win with this crowd. I pick up the money on Table 7 and can tell right away they didn't leave me a tip. Like I work for free. Through the window I see Silas Marner and his cohorts waiting for the Mercedes or Cadillac or BMW that they bought with money they should have rightfully left for tips. I can just imagine how many hardworking people have been stiffed by these penny-pinching potbellied pigs. That's it. I've had it. It is up to me to avenge this crime. I stride out the door, the money left for the bill wadded in my hand, and get right in Mr. Toupee's face.

"Excuse me, but did you get everything you ordered?"

Surprised, he answers, "Of course."

"Did I neglect you in any way? Did you have to wait long to be served? Was your food cold? The bathroom dirty? Did I have B.O.?"

The Wigman's friends start to sweat. They know they have finally been nabbed for robbery, so turn away and start birdwatching.

"It's not a law that I have to tip you, miss. You get a salary just like everyone else. Now, excuse me."

"What, you think I became a waitress for the glamour of minimum wage, no health insurance, and the chance to wait on an asshole like you?"

Rughead is apoplectic. "Why don't you get back inside before I call your manager!"

"Why don't you go to the Hair Club for Men and get a wig that actually matches your hair?"

"You, young lady, are getting fired. How dare you talk to me like that!"

"You know what? Take your fucking money back. I don't want it." I shove the money in his hands. "And stay the fuck away from here, okay?"

At that moment, the valet pulls his Jag up front. Wouldn't you know it? He stomps off to his car, throwing the money all over the sidewalk. His companions slink along behind him. He guns the engine and squeals down the street.

"Go to hell, you stupid asshole!"

Incautious? Possibly. But no bystanders were present. I wouldn't have had the guts to say any of that in front of witnesses. It'll be his word against mine; and waiters, like cops, look after their own. I march into the restaurant and head straight for the bar.

"Luis, give me a Kamikaze. And make it a double."

Vengeance is mine.

❖　❖　❖

When I get home, I see my answering machine flashing furiously. I turn it on and listen while I wash the grease off my face.

"Mutt? It's me. Call me at the restaurant, okay? Bye."

Jeff's working the noon-to-five shift. I'll call him when he gets home. Except, maybe he's calling me because I'm being fired.

Oh, God. I can't be fired.

A second message comes on. Jeff again. "Mutt? Pick up the phone; you're not going to believe what just happened. Hello? Damn!"

That's it; I'm history. I slowly dial the number.

"Mexicali Joe's, can I help you?"

I cringe at the manager's voice.

"Um, hi, it's Mutt. Can I talk to Jeff?"

The death knell is coming. Why did I shoot off my mouth? Why can't I be a better person?

"Mutt, I need to talk to you."

"Look, I didn't mean to. I'm really sorry."

"You know the rules. You're not supposed to call other employees while they're working."

"I know, I couldn't control my—what? Oh, yeah, I'm sorry."

A miracle. Thank you God. As penance, I'll go to church every day and volunteer at a nursing home.

"And I wondered if you could cover a five-to-midnight shift on Friday."

"Sure, of course, I'd be happy to! Thank you so much!"

"All right, I'll transfer you to Jeff. Remember the policy, okay?"

I genuflect twenty times while I'm on hold. Jeff picks up.

"Mutt, wait till you hear this! I just got invited to a party being hosted by your favorite fantasy."

"What?! You did? You don't even know her."

"I work out sometimes with this guy, Rick, who, it turns out, is a business associate of hers. Anyway, they came in together after you left, and Rick asked me if I would like to come to a party on Saturday at Allison's."

"Her name is Allison?"

"Yeah. So, I want to know if you'll go with me. As kind of a late birthday present. And Mark has a scene study class."

"What kind of party? I mean, what am I supposed to wear? I mean, no, I can't go."

"Mutt, you're going, okay? Wear something nice and I'll pick you up at 8:30. Saturday."

"Jeff, I—"

"I have to go; I just got three new tables. See you."

Allison. Her name is Allison. I am going to a party at Allison's. Wow.

I look through my drawers for anything that would be appropriate for a party at the house of a woman whom I don't know. Jeans. Jeans. Black jeans. Jean shorts. Jeans with holes. Better check the closet. Let's see, five white button-down work shirts, all stained. A denim shirt. A sleeveless denim shirt. I am fucked. My wardrobe's a dead giveaway that I am a representative of the underclass. I'll be a peasant eating at the table of the great and powerful Allison, who most likely will wear white linen and pearls.

I think I'll put a note on my door that I'm not at home, then hide in the closet when Jeff comes to get me. It won't work: he has a key and will know exactly where to find me.

Okay, I'll wear black jeans, the denim shirt, and a white tank. Luckily, I have my Tony Lamas to dress things up. I glued the rip, so it barely shows.

Oh, my God, I'm going to Allison's. How in the world can I get through the next thousand hours?

CHAPTER 7

God, it's crowded at the restaurant tonight. I jostle my way through a group of giggly women ordering margaritas up at the bar. There's not an empty stool in sight, with people doing the typical Friday night two-fisted drinking.

The evening flows by in a sea of food and faces. I'm glad I'm not a regular night waiter. Too much stress. Although I am happy for the extra money, since my rent is three days late.

Along about midnight, when quiet finally descends, I slide on my jean jacket and start for the door. I approach a straggler up at the bar, tap her shoulder, and say, "We're closed now."

The woman swivels in her seat to face me. It's Diane.

"Oh, uh, hi, Diane. How are you? You know, we're closed."

"I saw you at Out and About on Wednesday."

"Yeah, you had a reading. How'd it go?"

"Didn't you hear me calling you?"

"Gee . . . no." I dig the key to my bike lock out of my jacket pocket. "Well, see ya around."

"Do you want to go out for a drink?" she asks.

"Not really. I've had about as much noise as I can take."

Diane walks toward me and says, "Well, how about a drink at my house? It's close."

"I don't know; I'm kinda tired." Actually, I need my beauty sleep, so I'll be ready for the Allison Wonderland party tomorrow night.

"Come on, just one?"

"Well—"

"One drink and I promise to let you go in a half hour."

"You're very persistent."

"I'm sorry. I'm pushy, I know." She laughs lightly, shakes her head, then stares at me with bright and expectant eyes. "One drink? Please?"

"Well, since you put it so sweetly . . ."

"Great!"

We walk out to the street. As I unlock my bike, I say, "There's one ground rule. We can't talk about college, okay?"

"Okay. Hey, why don't we put your bike in the back of my Jeep?"

"All right."

We don't talk as we drive the few blocks to her house. I'm surprised that the silence actually feels companionable. We pull up to a small, white adobe house, the kind you see on practically every L.A. street. These homes were the preferred tract housing of the thirties, almost southwestern, but definitely with a hint of large-scale suburbia lurking in their boxy lines.

I sink into an overstuffed teal couch that begs me to close my eyes and sleep. Diane brings out a bottle of white wine and a plate of cheese and crackers. She puts on a CD of the Indigo Girls, setting the volume low. After pouring the wine, she sits at the other end of the couch.

"I'm so glad you came over," she says.

"Anytime."

"You know, I don't want to call you Mutt. Can I call you Muriel?"

Startled, I ask, "How did you remember my name?"

"I looked in a yearbook. But I'm not supposed to talk about college, so I won't. You were going to ride your bike home at midnight?"

"Well, I could have taken the bus, but have you ever been on an L.A. bus at night?"

"No."

"Let's just say it would be safer to stand naked at the corner of Hollywood and Vine."

I expect a laugh, which I don't get. Instead, I get a stare that's far too intense for my tastes.

"Do you have family in the area?" she asks.

"Nope. I have a Stepford sister in Modesto. We don't talk much. So, do you like teaching at PCC?"

"I love it. Next semester, I'm adding a class in 'Understanding Modern Poetry'."

"That's good."

"Help yourself to the cheese and crackers," she says.

"Okay."

"When did you move to L.A., Muriel?"

Muriel? Oh, Muriel. She means me. I've gotten so used to Mutt.

"Um, three years ago this April. How about you?"

"I moved back here after graduating last year."

"Weren't you in my class?"

"It took me a few years to get a Master's and teaching credentials."

I'm getting a sore neck from craning to look at her from my end of the couch, and a headache from the polite and superficial conversation.

"Why did you invite me over here, Diane?" I blurt out. I guess the headache has made me bold. Or rude.

"Why not?"

"'Why not?' That's an answer? You don't know me at all. I just, I just don't get it."

"Ever since that night at the Rifle, you've been on my mind," she says, smiling. Her dimples are disconcerting. Her arms, in a sea green tank top, stand out, healthy and defined. Then she shakes her hair, letting the curls fall around her face, and she's so cute, I think I want to kiss her. I stand up quickly and lean against the wall by the fireplace.

"Do you ever have occasion to use this?" I ask, nodding towards the fireplace.

"Sure. A couple times a year."

Silence drapes the room. I look at Diane's curls. She looks at my mouth. I look at my feet. So does she.

I break the stillness. "So, what's the deal?"

"Deal? What deal?"

"Yeah, like, what's going on here?"

"I just want to get to know you better. That's all. Frankly, I wanted to get to know you better in school."

"To be honest, I only vaguely remember you from school."

"I remember you. God, did I have a crush on you!"

"You're kidding! Why?"

"I don't know. Who can explain crushes? They're not based on any sense of reality. They just happen. I ended up having an affair, if you could call it that, with one of my professors. I never even talked to you. You were so unapproachable at the time. You seemed so . . . I don't know, disaffected."

Wow, an affair with a professor. Life does imitate lesbian novels. I move back to the couch, with the confidence of being the object of a crush.

"Do I seem so unapproachable now?"

"You're in my house."

"I guess so. Do you mind if I smoke?"

Diane reaches behind her to open a window and says, "It's fine." She gets up and opens two other windows. Obviously, she does mind if I smoke.

"That's okay," I say, "I don't need to. You don't have to open any more windows."

She perches on the arm of a matching chair and asks, "Why were you so hard to talk to in school?"

"Me?"

"Were you shy?"

"I was having an identity crisis. My sister forced me to go to school. I wanted to work at the animal shelter. But Sister Sandra said that Mom's dying wish was for me to be a college graduate. So I went. You can't argue with the wishes of the dead. Although I argued a lot with Sandra the Undead."

"I'm sorry about your mom."

"I'm over it."

"Are you . . . God, I'm going to sound pushy again."

"What?"

She clears her throat and asks, "Are you seeing anyone?"

"Me? Hah! That's funny."

"Are you?"

"No."

"Good." Diane gives me a mischievous look.

"Um, it's getting late. I really need to go."

"I won't let you ride your bike home. I'll drive you."

"No, it's okay. I'm fine."

"Look, you can have another glass of wine; I'll drive you home, and you'll still be there sooner than if you biked."

"Okay." Who can argue with that kind of logic?

"So, why don't you take off your jacket?"

"All right."

Diane walks over and helps me take it off. She's standing really close to me. I mean, really close. I can see flecks of brown floating like islands in her blue eyes. I step back, scared of her closeness, and more scared of the look in her eyes. I ask where I can hang the jacket.

"Hang it on that coat rack to your right."

"The one that is eighteen inches from my face? Duh." I hang up the jacket, then sit back down.

"Let's listen to something different," Diane says.

"Okay. Do you have any Fleetwood Mac?"

"Sorry."

Diane replaces the Girls with Lena Horne. This is starting to feel like a seduction. She's got that ready-for-the-hunt look, eyes narrowed and focused.

"You seem a little tense," she murmurs, then proceeds to rub my shoulders.

This *is* a seduction.

I'm on the floor; she's on the couch, and I let her massage my back. It feels really good. Then I feel her lips on my neck. I don't quite believe this. Just don't kiss my ear. It's all over if you kiss my ear.

Her hands stroke my back in slow circles. I lean my head forward, so she feels free to keep kissing my neck. She slides off the couch so that she's next to me, and turns my head toward her.

Staring at my lips, she whispers, "God, you're beautiful."

I swallow hard, try to keep breathing, and our lips meet. Her mouth opens under mine, and we kiss deeply. I wrap my hands in her hair; she caresses my breast through my shirt. She kisses my cheek, my forehead, my lips again. She tugs at my shirt, trying to get it out of my jeans. When she does, she moves her hand along my rib cage to my breast. I nestle my head in her neck and breathe in her scent. She smells so good: fresh and clean. Her soft face belies her muscular legs. I run my hand along her flushed, warm skin.

I watch her begin to unbutton my shirt, but freeze when I see the front of it all splattered with salsa and guacamole. Shit. I must smell like rotten food.

I stop her hands and say, "This shirt is filthy. I'm filthy."

"You're fine."

"I can't do this. I'm covered in fajita juice."

"Take off your shirt. You're fine."

She continues unbuttoning, then slides the shirt from my body. I help her with my bra. She lays me down on the floor and presses her lips against my chest. My thoughts are now totally tuned to my body, which is, to be frank, very happy doing its own thing.

She keeps kissing my breasts while she runs her hand up the inside of my thigh. Through my jeans, I feel her hand move between my legs, and she starts rubbing slowly. She stops to take off her T-shirt.

My body may be thoroughly enjoying this, but my head suddenly snaps into something completely different: I don't know this woman at all. We just met. I don't understand what she likes about me. Am I too easy? Is this just a one-night stand for her? She seems so nice.

I sit up. I'm breathing really hard. I calm myself and say, "This is freaking me out. I don't know if this is the right thing to do."

Diane strokes my leg and says, "Does it make you feel good?"

"I don't know. Yes."

"Then it's the right thing to do." She kisses me again, then puts her tongue in my ear.

Oh, man. I told her not to do that.

❖   ❖   ❖

I can't sleep. It's 3:30 a.m. I need to work tomorrow. I mean, today. I don't have any clean clothes. Diane turns over and lays her hand on my stomach. I hope she's asleep. Yeah—rhythmic breathing. Why didn't I go home?

This bed is too firm. I've got a backache, among other aches. The room smells of sex. I'm getting turned on again. I feel guilty for being turned on. Where's the off switch?

Where are my morals? And my comfortable bed? What am I gonna do for clothes? What am I gonna do with Diane?

Oh, she's nice, she's sweet, she's completely and entirely sexy. She likes me; I mean, she calls me by my real name. I hate that I'm awake. I hate to feel bad about this.

I'll just count backwards from 100 until I fall asleep. 100. 99. 98. I can't believe I'm in this bed. 100. 99. 98. 97. 96. 95. 94 . . .

❖   ❖   ❖

I'm startled awake by the phone jangling right next to my head. Diane leans over me to pick it up. Her breast grazes my cheek, and I turn my head to kiss it. I mean, it's right there; what else can I do?

She sits up next to me. I roll over to face her, and she absentmindedly plays with a strand of my hair.

"Hello? Oh, hi. Yeah, hold on, I'll grab the phone in the other room." Diane hands me the phone and whispers, "Hang up when I'm on the other line, okay?"

"Okay."

She throws on a robe that she's taken from behind the door, then says, "I left out a shirt for you. I'm washing your clothes so they'll be clean for work. And there's coffee in the kitchen."

I hang up the phone when I hear her on the other end. I grab the shirt from the end of the bed. It's a pink T-shirt that would probably look fine on Barbie, but I'm having a hard time squeezing it on. Oh, yeah, nice—it only comes to my stomach. Now what do I do? My sense of calm is quickly dissipating into panic.

You ever dream you're naked and have to deal with people in a competent, adult manner? Am I supposed to walk confidently out to the kitchen and pour myself a cup of coffee with my pubes showing? I don't think so.

I'll just see if there's another robe on the door. I pull the shirt down as far as it will go and sprint for the doorway. No luck. Okay, I'll check her drawers for some shorts or, at the bare minimum, underwear. Is that considered criminal trespassing? What if Diane walks in and my hands are deep in her underwear drawer?

I guess the only thing I can do is sit on the bed, pull the sheet over my lap, and wait for Chatty Cathy to return. I give her room a visual once-over for any possible hints of a personality disorder.

To my right, double French doors look out on a small yard with sun-browned grass. There's a lemon tree, an orange tree, and the ubiquitous waxy, tangerine-hued bird of paradise, with its flower that can gouge an eye out. Across from me stands a tall, antique rosewood dresser that fits snugly between the hall door and the closet door. The top holds hand-blown glass bottles, some squat and glazed purple with age, others new and angular and brightly tinted in yellows and oranges. To my left runs a low, wall-to-wall bookcase. Above it hangs a mirror in which I startle at my own image. What am I doing in this strange place?

She has 100% cotton sheets, 100% down pillows, and a 100% down comforter. The eggshell white walls suffer spidery cracks where the ceiling and wall join. This joint survived the earthquake in style; my tomb has a floor-to-ceiling crack that you can stick two fingers in. And the apartment manager tells me there's no structural damage. Yeah, right.

I see no obvious signs of mental illness or schizophrenia. In fact, if there's one thing I can say about Diane, it's that she seems totally normal and together, with good, if slightly predictable, tastes.

Well, enough of the *Better Homes and Gardens* tour that took approximately seventeen seconds. Get off the phone, Diane. I want coffee.

And I want my pants.

CHAPTER 8

Allison lives in Beverly Hills, in a house set far back from the road, tucked amidst a myriad of greenery. It takes Jeff and me ten minutes to walk up the driveway full of Porsches, Jeeps, and other expensive cars. As we cross a rounded Japanese bridge to reach the open double doors, the sounds of a small string ensemble play somewhere in front of us. This is Wonderland, not Muttland. I bet my apartment could fit inside the kitchen pantry.

Oh, man, am I underdressed. Of course, Jeff looks fantastic in a double-breasted suit. He always looks fantastic. We wade through groups of perfectly coifed people, and I pick up bits and pieces of conversations.

". . . so, I transferred from Sony Classics to MGM, which was a big mistake, believe me . . ."

". . . Meryl didn't want . . ."

". . . they butchered my script, and cast a *soap star* in the lead . . ."

". . . twenty fucking million dollars, down the . . ."

Caterers mill through the crowd, serving good-looking, bad-tasting tidbits. But, then again, I could never get into that fish egg thing. Jeff finds Rick, and I am suddenly a speck of dust in their eyes. I scan the room for Allison, but a lanky woman with long crimson nails and even longer fuchsia hair blocks my view.

"So, who are you with?" she asks.

"Excuse me?"

"I'm with All Girls."

"Oh." Hmmm. Is this a come-on?

"I'm looking to join Disney's marketing team," she continues, "but it's a bitch to break in."

"Yeah, I bet that's hard."

Jeff and Rick have forgotten about me and have joined a group of men by the fireplace.

Extending a well-manicured hand, Miss All Girls says, "I'm Caroline Lieberman."

"Nice to meet you," I say.

"And you said you were with . . . ?"

"I'm not exactly in the business," I answer.

"Oh. How lucky for you. Well, enjoy the party."

She fades away, like they do in *Star Trek* when the crew beams up from a hostile planet. I stand in the middle of the room, alone in a horde of networkers. Jeff is nowhere in sight.

I locate the string quartet, lean against a wall, and try to appear completely wrapped up in Mozart, or Schumann, or whoever the hell these guys are playing. I figure I'll stay locked in this position until Jeff decides to go. I take a glass of champagne from a tray discreetly placed in front of me. I recall that champagne must be sipped, so I am conscious of every swallow. I look at my watch; a whole twenty minutes have gone by. I'm only going to have to endure, oh, another three hours or so of this nonsense.

The musicians set down their instruments to take a break. Now what will I do? I pull a cigarette out of my breast pocket and dig my lighter out of my jeans. I pause to check for other smokers. Nope. Not a whiff of smoke in the air.

I walk towards the back of the house and find the patio. Sandstone, of course. I step out into the warm air and walk along the edge of the swimming pool. The lights in the pool give a golden cast to the oak trees and ferns that hug the patio. I sit on the edge of a lounge chair and light up. Now, this life I could get used to. I feel prosperous here, not surrounded by the anxiety of my own poverty. Well, if you grow up in a trailer with a view of the gas station, and your mother blows the welfare check playing bingo on the first of the month, poverty consciousness follows you like a hungry rat.

A breeze touches the water, and the ripples glint flaxen, then disappear. I sigh, relaxing deeper into the chair.

"Ah, fresh air."

I practically jump out of my boots; I didn't expect anyone else to be out here. I turn my head and there stands Allison, her face lit by the soft glow. She's exquisite. I swear that's the only word for her. She looks at me, and her brow furrows in puzzlement.

I say hurriedly, "I didn't crash your party. Your friend, Rick, invited my friend Jeff, who invited me, which I suppose comes close to 'crashing,' but—"

She laughs and sits on the next lounge chair.

"Could I have one of your cigarettes? I don't really smoke, but I'm feeling decadent."

"Yeah, sure." My hands shake as I get her the cigarette, and I drop my lighter under the lounge chair. God, I'm a schmuck. I retrieve the Bic and try not to scorch her hair as I give her a light.

"Mmmm. Good," she says. "You work at that Mexican restaurant, right? And so does—"

"Jeff. Yeah."

"Having a nice time?"

"Well—"

"Obviously not, or you wouldn't be hiding out here in the ferns."

"No, I'm having a great time."

"Well, I'm having a miserable time. Which is why I, too, am hiding out in the ferns."

"But aren't these all your friends?"

"Friends? No, they're my clients. And my clients' clients. What did you say your name was?"

"I'm, um, Mutt."

"Mutt?"

"Mutt."

"Oh, I get it. Mutt and Jeff? That's amusing . . ."

Allison seems to be thoroughly enjoying her smoke and takes her time finishing it.

"I like your house," I say. "It's got nice lines."

She purses her lips, and her eyebrows meet in thought. "Best thing about my divorce. Where do you live?"

"Los Feliz."

"Nice area. Do you live with someone?"

"No. I had a cat once, but it didn't work out."

"I live alone, too. I got divorced over a woman. That I was seeing. Turns out she was having an affair with my husband, and when he left, so did she. Sort of. Tawdry, tawdry, tawdry."

"Wow, I'm sorry."

"I'm not."

The string quartet starts up again, and muffled Haydn floats quietly out the door.

"So, Mutt. What else do you do besides waitressing?"

"I just waitress."

"How interesting. All the waiters I know write screenplays, or act, or go to school. Are you a student?"

"Nope. I graduated from San Jose State with a B.S. in anthropology."

"Ooh, anthropology."

"I know. Bad major."

"Do you act? You're pretty enough."

"No, really, I'm just a waiter."

"Do you know how rare and refreshing that is? You're who you are, no apologies. No bullshit. Now, those people..." She points a finger towards her house. "Now that is bullshit. That is back-stabbing bullshit. Those people just pretend to be people."

Allison stands up and moves over to my lounge chair. She places a hand on my shoulder to steady herself and sits heavily by my side.

"I'll tell you a little secret, because I'm a tiny bit tipsy right now, and prone to telling the truth. I hate those people. But you, *you*. Do you know how sexy just being a waitress can be?" She stares at me, her gaze steady, though her body sways slightly. She tilts her head to one side. "Life can be very simple sometimes, can't it?"

"I'm not sure what you mean."

"May I kiss you?"

I almost fall off the chair. Allison, my fantasy, wants to kiss me. She looks at me with such great seriousness, like, if I said no, she might crumble into nothingness. Can I say no to such a look? I don't think so.

Suddenly, she kisses me. She has her hand on my cheek and her lips are so soft. I pull her closer. I'm not a fool. I'll take advantage of this once-in-an-eon opportunity.

"A sweet, simple kiss," she whispers, her breath warm on my lips. "Just what I needed."

The music suddenly becomes louder, and a strong shadow falls out the patio door.

"Allie?" It's a woman's voice, and it does not sound pleased.

Allison abruptly sits up, then puts her head in her hands. "What am I doing?" She stands and says, "Sorry. I'm drunk."

She walks to the patio door and, without looking back, murmurs, "Have a good time at the party." Then she slides the door shut behind her.

I lean back against my chair, look up at the stars, and wipe my nose on the back of my hand. I breathe slowly in and out. This evening is like a movie. This evening is like being kissed by Greta Garbo. This evening is like a dream: a bizarre, strange dream.

I really don't know how that happened. That kiss. I didn't do it. I suppose that I was in the right place at the very right time. If only we hadn't been interrupted.

I put my hands up to my burning cheeks. Oh, my God, I have been kissed by Allison. Wait until I tell Jeff.

CHAPTER 9

It's been three days since I tumbled so willingly into bed with Diane, and two days since the kiss that shifted my life. Allison hasn't called me; I didn't expect she would. But I did expect Diane to call. I think she's embarrassed about washing my red socks with my white shirt. Now, big splotches of red dot the shirt, which make it look like a multiple knifing has taken place.

The kitchen at Mexicali Joe's is being renovated, because the stoves didn't pass fire code, so all the waiters have the next two days off. We decide as a group to "bond," and a majority (in other words, the night waiters) votes to go to the zoo, then have a barbecue at Denise's house.

The zoo does not fit my idea of a good time. Let's talk about animal cruelty. Stripping a baby gorilla from its mother's arms, killing the mother as she tries to defend her family, and carting the baby off to a 6x8-foot cage to be gawked at and teased? Now, that's cruel.

And the L.A. Zoo takes the cake on faux-reality ridiculousness. It has this exhibit on kiwis and koalas, but instead of just letting these animals be the nightcrawlers they are, the zoo architects have constructed a windowless building that "simulates" the nighttime light and approximate temperature of the Continent Down Under. In addition, some non-union set decorators have added a mural that "mimics" a eucalyptus forest. Now, forgive me, but the designers of the Lawrence Welk set did a better job than these bozos.

As we walk through the section on Africa, I have this incredible urge to open every gate and cage. Animals should be in the wild, not stolen for posterity. The only thing that stops me from liberating the beasts is the fact that they would make rush hour tougher than it already is.

❖   ❖   ❖

Later, at the barbecue, Jeff and I squeeze into a corner between the couch and a wall. Everyone tries their best to have a good time, evidenced by the free-flowing margaritas, tequila, and beer. You would think, working at a Mexican restaurant, we would all be tired of margaritas, tequila, and beer. Go figure.

"Jeff," I proclaim, "I think we're headed for an era of religious fascism."

"No way! Our government is set up to keep the left and right equal."

"Our founding fathers created a balance of powers, that's true. But—and this is a big 'but'—that balance is ruled by the whim of the people, who, unfortunately, have swung to the far right. The Democrats might as well pack their bags and go home."

"Who has a big butt?"

"Hello? Are you even listening to me?"

"Yeah, yeah."

"Good. See, if the liberals can move the government back to center, we'll be A-okay. In the meantime, the underclass and the disabled will have hell to pay."

God, I'm smart after a couple lines of coke. This is great: I didn't know this stuff could make me an intellectual. And sober.

Jeff stretches out his legs and leans against the couch. "I don't know," he answers, "I don't really care about politics. I'd rather live my own life and let everything else be. There's nothing I can do about it."

"Of course there is!" I kneel beside him. "You write your legislators, you become an activist, you make your voice known!"

"Like you?"

"Well, someday I will."

"Uh-huh," Jeff says, a skeptical look on his face.

"I will!"

"Yeah, right. Come on, Mutt. I love you and all, but you're not an activist."

"I could be. Hey, I send money to PETA."

"And I bet they love those black leather boots of yours."

I shut my mouth. He's right. I'm an apathetic hypocrite living in a piece-of-shit apartment in a cesspool of a city.

"I'm a loser," I say. "You're right. I have no purpose."

"Well, I'm totally comfortable living a purposeless life."

"Maybe if we had purpose, we'd be happy."

"I'm happy. I have a job, a lover, good friends—"

"That's more than I have," I mutter. "I'm a pseudo-intellectual who'll never amount to anything, and no one likes me."

"Don't go overboard, Mutt. I love you."

"I know, but you're a *guy*."

"So that makes my love worthless?"

"No, that's not—"

"What about What's-Her-Name? Diane. She likes you."

"She ruined my shirt."

"So what?"

"She hasn't called me."

"Why don't you call her?"

"It was a one-night stand. Besides, I have my mind set on other things."

"I don't believe you sometimes."

"I can't help who I love."

"Oh, now you love Allison? You've talked to her once! You are out of control. How about some more coke, or something to drink?"

"No. I'm too depressed now. I think I'm gonna go home."

"You want a ride?"

"It's only six blocks away."

"Don't get so depressed. Look, you have a job, you have me—"

I brush off the seat of my pants and say, "Yeah, that's cool. But you know what I really want? Purpose."

Jeff gets up, rolling his eyes. I follow him to the kitchen. All the other waitrons have moved to the den to watch an action-adventure psycho-thriller.

"How's Mark?" I ask, mostly because I don't want to talk about me anymore.

"He's all right. He's really unhappy living here. He wants to move to Chicago to get some acting work that pays."

"You guys aren't going, are you?" I ask, turning cold with panic.

"I don't know. We're looking into it."

"But you're my anchor! You can't go. I don't fucking believe this."

"We probably won't go. Like I said, we're just checking it out. Don't worry, Mutt."

I step outside, surprised that it's still light out. I look at my watch: 7:12 p.m. I can't believe it's so early. I can't believe Jeff may be leaving me. I can't believe I thought coke was great. Now all I have is a headache, and I feel like I'm going to have a heart attack.

After grabbing my mail, I run up the stairs and do a face plant against my door. Damn, what the hell tripped me? I guess I should have bought a new bulb when the old one burned out last Christmas. Swinging my door open, I flip on a light and scan the landing. A package. Please God, Sister Sandra didn't send me more summer dresses with Peter Pan collars, did she? I know, appreciate the thought, not the gift, but really. I take the box inside, set it on top of the TV, and flip on "Nick at Nite," my comfort television. You can't beat reruns of 70s TV. Yes! It's Mary, who can turn the world on with her smile. Grabbing the box, I plop on the couch/bed and look for a return address, which I don't find. Definitely not Sis's style. I tear open the package and pull out two white button-down shirts. There's a card on the bottom of the box, and a big manila envelope. I open the card:

Dear Muriel,
I'm sorry about your shirt. I hope these fit.
Thanks for an incredible evening. I've included some poetry; I'd love to know what you think.
Can we get together soon? Call me.
    Love, D.
    P.S. You are very sexy.

Wow, she didn't have to get me these shirts. That was really nice. Overkill, but nice.

I am about to toss all the junk mail out, when my eye stops on an actual handwritten letter. Heavy linen card stock. Subdued, yet elegant. I carefully tear open the envelope and slide out the card.

> I want to apologize for Saturday
> night. Could I make it up to you
> by taking you out to dinner?
>
> Allison O'Malley

Oh, my God.

I reread the note. Five times. Just for clarity. Allison O'Malley wants to take me to dinner. Oh, my God. I hold my chest; my heart is about to beat out of my chest cavity. I can't tell if the pain is coming from the note or the illegal drugs. How did she get my address? I can't keep obsessing about this, or I'll have a coronary.

I know: I'll read Diane's poetry. I pull out the first one: "For the Girl in Humanities Rm 102." It's all about unrequited love and lost souls and Lilith and Artemis. I don't quite get the goddess connection, but it sure sounds like a love poem. Like a love poem to me.

I shake my head in total disbelief. I can't handle this. What, does she want to register at Nordstrom's after one date? Typically lesbo.

Allison wants dinner. Diane wants a wedding (if I understood her poem). What would Mary Richards do in this conundrum? She'd talk to Murray.

I pick up the phone and dial Jeff.

CHAPTER 10

THE DINNER is tonight. Allison should be here in twenty minutes. She insisted on picking me up, but I'm too embarrassed for her to see my apartment, so I plan to wait for her outside. An eighteenth-century miner's tenement would be a step up from this dump. I recheck myself in the mirror. Not bad. The hair looks good, and the linen shirt and pants that I dumped a week of tips into certainly do the trick. I head for the door, but as my hand grabs the knob, I hear a knock on the other side. Oh, God, she's early. I'm sunk. I take three deep breaths and open the door.

In a tinny, bright voice, I say, "Hi, Allis—Diane?"

"I was in the neighborhood, so I thought I'd stop by."

"Oh, that's great."

"You look incredible," she says.

"Yeah? Thanks." I feel like the cat caught with the proverbial bird. I close and lock the door behind me, pointedly looking at my watch. Diane leans forward and kisses me. Damn, I hope my lipstick didn't smear.

"Gee, Diane, I'm just heading out to meet a . . . friend. Sorry. Otherwise, I'd have invited you in."

"It's okay," she says. Do her shoulders have to slump quite so forlornly? "Like I said, I was in the neighborhood."

"Are you all right? Your face just got really flushed."

"Is it?" she asks, putting a hand to her cheek. "No, I'm fine. It's hot on this landing. I guess I'll be going."

She turns and walks down the stairs, like a puppy who has just been rejected by her mother. Why do I feel so guilty? I take the stairs two at a time to catch up with her.

"Listen, Diane, let's meet later in the week for coffee or something, okay?"

As we head towards the sidewalk, Diane says, "Muriel, if you don't want to see me, I'll understand."

"That's ridiculous!" I exclaim, scanning the street for Allison.

"Really?"

"Yeah, I mean it. Let's meet for coffee."

Diane blasts me with her eye-popping smile. As we give each other an awkward hug, a white Mercedes pulls up next to us. My dinner date. I step away from Diane and say, "Well, gotta go."

Like Venus rising from the depths of the sea, Allison steps out of the car and heads towards us. Well, past me and towards Diane. She extends her hand and says, "I enjoyed your reading. You're very talented."

"Really? Thank you so much."

"Do you have a publisher?"

"No, I'm working on getting an agent right now."

"I may know someone. Let me get you my card; I have the number at work."

Diane follows Allison around the driver's side of the car.

"I'm Allison O'Malley."

"Diane Ellis."

"Yes, I know."

"Of course," Diane laughs.

Hello? Remember me? Mutt, your date? Mutt, the loser? Jesus. I could be on a different planet from these two. They exchange numbers, cards, and other vital statistics, like their astrological signs. Finally, after they've discussed past lives, the two notice me.

"Have fun!" Diane says.

"Thanks."

I turn to find Allison already waiting in the car. She reaches over and pushes open my door. When I slide onto the black leather seat and then off the seat into the console, I catch her waving at Diane. I kind of resent them both right now. But I really resent smooth leather.

As I right myself, Allison pulls the car onto the street and says, "I thought we'd go to Luigi's in Old Town. Okay with you?"

"That sounds great. Where's Old Town?"

She looks at me as if I'd asked who Santa Claus was. "In Pasadena."

"Oh, right. Pasadena. Never been there."

We're on the 210 freeway, speeding east. Even though there are probably ten lanes for either direction of traffic, we get stuck in one of SoCal's perpetual traffic jams. It doesn't bother me, though: I'll sit in an air-conditioned Mercedes any day of the week.

We park the car in Old Town, then Allison strides down the street, three paces ahead of me. I have to run to keep up. She passes a line of about thirty people, hands the maitre d' a twenty-dollar bill, and he whisks us to a private booth. This place gleams with polished mahogany, brass, cut glass, and money. The waiters waft, silent and somber, from table to table. They probably get fired for talking. I'll bet it would be easier for me to get a job with the CIA than with Luigi's.

Allison orders a bottle of Chianti, Caesar salads, an eggplant parmesan for her, and fettucine Alfredo for me. Wow, I didn't even have to open my menu. I feel spoiled. The wine steward pours a drop of Chianti into Allison's glass. She twirls the dark liquid, smells it, rolls a bit on her tongue. The steward and I lean forward in anticipation. Will the wine pass? It does; we breathe a collective sigh of relief.

When the steward leaves, Allison says, "A toast. To mending mistakes."

"Thanks for bringing me here. It's a beautiful restaurant."

"They have wonderful food. You'll see. Would you like to smoke?"

"Sure."

"May I have one, too?"

I thought she "really didn't smoke." Whatever. We sit, smoking, and sipping our authentic Italian wine, but this fifty-dollar bottle doesn't taste any different to me than the six-dollar stuff with the screw cap.

"You know, Mutt, I have to apologize for my behavior at the party. It was entirely inappropriate, and I'm very sorry."

"It's okay."

"No, it's not. I took advantage of you."

"Really, it's okay. Don't worry about it."

"Enough said." She runs her finger around the lip of her wine glass; she has such beautiful hands, elegant and careful.

"So, tell me about yourself," she continues.

"There's not much to tell. I work as a waitress; I live in Los Feliz. That's about it."

"That can't be all. Are you from L.A. originally?"

"I'm from Castroville."

"Castroville? Ah, yes, the artichoke capital."

"You got it."

"Do you still have family up there?"

"No. I have a sister in Modesto. Sandra Dee."

"That's her real name?"

"That's her name."

"And your parents?"

"They're dead."

"I'm so sorry," she murmurs.

"Nah, it's okay. Actually, I never knew my father. He got killed on a construction site when I was a couple months old. My mom, my sister, and I lived with my grandma until she passed away; then my mom got sick. I looked after her until she died."

"When was that?"

"When I was twenty. I went to college after that."

"My God, that must have been hard on you."

"I don't know. It was hard to lose my mom. But it was a relief, also."

"I've heard that before."

"Yeah, it's true. I don't know why I'm telling you all this. What about your folks?"

"They live in Palm Springs."

"Do you see them a lot?"

"Christmas and birthdays."

"Do you have any brothers or sisters?"

"One brother. Michael. He's an accountant in Boston. He's wonderful. I miss him very much."

Our salads arrive, crisp leaves stacked high and crowned with a single anchovy, which I slide to the side of my plate. Allison orders another bottle of wine.

"You said everyone at your party was a client of yours?" I ask.

"I'm an entertainment lawyer. I never thought I'd be doing this, but I make good money."

"What did you want to do?"

"Oh, be an artist, I suppose. Although my paintings were terrible. And Dad would only pay for medical or law school."

"You could still be an artist."

"I don't think so. It's a dead dream. I'm stuck where I am. What about you?"

"Me?"

"What did you want to be when you grew up?"

"Somebody else."

Allison stops eating, fork midway to her mouth, and gives me a funny look that I can't quite figure out. Then a corner of her mouth turns up and she says, "I hope, someday, you get to be that 'someone else.'"

We pass the rest of the meal in small talk, quickly swimming out of the vortex of truth. Allison tells of still working with her husband, although their offices lie at separate ends of the hall. She attended Yale and is thirty-nine. She hates Hollywood, with all the backstabbing and lies.

I'm acutely aware of the embarrassing spectacle I must seem to her. My hair is sloppy. I'm using the wrong fork. Even my new linen shirt and slacks now look crinkled and slovenly. I wanted to impress her. Instead, I remind myself of Cousin It. Why am I always a pretender at the ball?

❖   ❖   ❖

When we arrive in front of my apartment, Allison leaves the engine running.

"Thank you for a lovely dinner," she says.

"Thank *you*."

"I'll see you at the restaurant, then?"

"Great."

She holds out her hand, we shake, and I get out of the car.

"Oh," I lean back in to say, "you know, my name is really Muriel."

"Well, Muriel, thank you again. You're, I don't know, so refreshing."

I watch her drive away, until her taillights disappear around the corner. I head for my studio, practically walking on air. Allison is sophisticated, polished, intelligent, nice— and I was lucky enough to have dinner with her.

I carefully hang my outfit in the closet, so I can return it to Nordstrom's tomorrow. Switching to a T-shirt and jeans, I head toward the TV and click on Nick. You know what? I don't even need Mary, Rhoda, or Murray tonight. I turn off the set, and stand looking out the window at the night sky. I never realized the city lights made the sky violet. What a beautiful color.

L.A.'s not so bad when you're in love.

CHAPTER 11

Jeff and I sit at the restaurant bar on what has to be the slowest day in the history of the world. There have been, no lie, only two tables of customers in the last four hours.

"I'm really depressed, Jeff."

"No tips?"

"No, because Allison hasn't come in."

"Maybe she's out of town."

"Or doesn't like me."

"Have you ever thought that it might not have been a date? That she was just making amends?"

"It was a date."

"You didn't kiss good night, right?"

I shake my head.

Jeff says, "Then it wasn't a date."

"Well, maybe she wants to go slow."

"Did she say that?"

"No, but—"

"To be honest, I think she's a little bit out of your league."

"How nice of you to share that," I answer.

"It's a fact, that's all."

"You know, Jeff, I have the distinct feeling you don't respect me anymore."

"Mutt—"

"People from different backgrounds fall in love all the time. Think of Romeo and Juliet. Tony and Maria. Lady and the Tramp. I don't need you spitting on my possibilities for advancement."

"Chill out. I'm just saying that it might not have been a date. Why don't you concentrate on Diane? She has the hots for you."

"For your information, I'm seeing her tomorrow. We're going to the Arboretum."

Jeff puts his hand to his chest and swoons. "Oh, my God, Pasadena! Not twice in your life. What's going on with you?"

"Wanna go?"

"No one goes to Pasadena."

"Hey, we could double date."

"Mutt!"

"What?"

"Don't you like Diane? Or is it that you can't see past your obsession with Ms. Beverly Hills?"

"No, Diane's all right."

"Just make sure you're not leading her on."

"I'm not! Look, I didn't ask her to keep calling me. I didn't ask her to care."

"Jesus, Mutt, sometimes I think you're ten years old."

"Can we end this conversation? Now?"

"Fine."

"Fine."

Jeff takes a sip of his soda, then starts playing with the straw, pushing it up and down through the ice. He is thoroughly irritating today.

"Hey, Jeff, wanna go to the Rifle tonight?"

Even though he bugs me, he's still my best buddy.

"Sorry. Mark and I have to look over our tour books on Chicago." He sighs until there's not an atom of air left in his lungs. Okay, so he's a tad overdramatic.

"Come on, you're going to look at books all night?"

"Mark's very serious about this. And he asked me to cut back on the late nights."

I smirk. "What, he put you on a leash?"

"No, Mutt! If you knew anything about relationships—which you don't—you'd know you have to compromise."

"You don't have to yell at me. I was just joking."

"No, you weren't. Mark said he'd leave me if we didn't start doing more together. He means a lot to me, okay?"

"Why doesn't he come to the Rifle with us? Then you'll be together."

"You know he hates bars."

"Then why's he working at the Butthole?"

"He likes it there."

"Oh, yeah, he loves the ambiance. I think he's limiting you."

"No, Mutt, we're compromising, get it?"

"Okay, okay, you're giving in, I mean, compromising. Sorry for the slip. But, Jeff, I don't want to lose you. And I don't think 'compromise' means getting dragged to Chicago."

"I know. But I don't want to lose Mark."

"Well, maybe the 'house arrest'—"

"Mutt!"

"Sorry. Maybe the 'house rules' will relax soon, and we can go out."

"Yeah."

"Yeah."

We're quiet for a minute. I grab him in a bear hug. Then I decide to be an adult and say the right thing. Much as it pains me.

"You know what, Jeff? I will support anything you want to do. I love you. And, hey, Chicago's supposed to be a great town."

"Anything's better than L.A., huh?"

"Absolutely."

"Thanks, Mutt."

"You're welcome."

I feel my heart drop. How can I lose my best friend?

CHAPTER 12

Diane looks at the splendid view out my window and smiles. "It's a perfect day for the Arboretum." I'm busy putting the bagels, lox, and cream cheese she brought over onto plates. She showed up here at 8:10 a.m.— two hours before she was slated to arrive. What an eager little beaver. She looks, however, absolutely adorable in her blue wool Yankees cap. I, on the other hand, look like, well, shit. I've got on last night's T-shirt, dirty jeans, and mismatched socks. 8:10 is just way too early for me. I set the food on the coffee table and go back to the kitchen area to pour some coffee.

"Thanks for bringing breakfast, Diane. But, I have to tell you, I was kind of surprised to see you so early."

"I know, I'm sorry. It's just that I went to a sunrise meditation circle at the LGBCTTT Reformed Church, and I thought, since I was already out—"

"The *what* church?"

"You know, the Lesbian/Gay/Bisexual/Curious/Transsexual/Transgendered/Transvestite Reformed Church on Beverly?"

"Sounds extremely inclusive."

"Yeah, there's a lot of unity among the members."

"What time was the meditation? 4:30 a.m?"

"No, I go to the Women-born Women Only circle at 6:00."

"So much for unity."

"What do you mean?"

"Nothing. Here's your coffee."

"Thanks." She takes a sip. "Mmm, French vanilla, my favorite."

The bagel and lox are heavenly. What a treat. Any residual resentment I had of Diane's early-morning arrival now vanishes.

"So," she says through bites, "I called your friend Allison, and she gave me the name of a literary agent to submit my work to."

"Oh?"

"She is so great."

"The agent?"

"Allison."

"Yeah, she's wonderful," I say between clenched teeth. Something about these two together really irks me.

"Did you get a chance to read what I sent you?"

"Um, I read the first one. It was interesting."

"That's what people say when they don't like something, but want to be nice."

"Really? I just thought it was interesting."

"So, where'd you go for dinner?" Diane asks, in an obvious bid for a subject change.

"Um, Luigi's. Did I hurt your feelings? I mean, the poem was good, I guess. I don't really know anything about poetry."

"No, no. It's okay. I'm sensitive, that's all. You don't have to read the rest."

"But I will. I want to," I say. Now *I* better change the subject. "Why did you want to go to the Arboretum?"

"It's a nice place to walk around. I brought my camera. I've been wanting to take some pictures of the tropical flowers."

"You're a photographer, too?"

"As a hobby."

"A Renaissance woman."

"No, I just like to do things that make me happy."

❖   ❖   ❖

And, as promised, I am standing around while Diane indulges in happiness. She's spent the last half hour photographing an orchid from every possible distance and angle. The humidity in the greenhouse makes me light-headed, and the heavy sweet scent of the flowers turns my stomach.

Diane aims her camera at me and asks, "Could you turn your head to the left? You have a great profile, and the light in here—"

"Don't take my picture. I hate pictures."

"Come on, it'll be fun."

"No, it won't. Trust me. Frizzy hair doesn't look . . ."

She snaps a picture as I'm mid-sentence. That'll be charming.

"Why'd you do that? I don't want my picture taken."

"Just one more, okay?"

"Diane, don't. I don't feel very good."

The room is starting to spin. I quickly sit down.

"It's so damn hot in here," I mumble.

"Muriel, are you okay?"

Diane crouches next to me, sets her camera down, and places the back of her hand on my forehead.

"I think you have a temperature. God, you look terrible."

Her voice fades into a thudding sound in my head. Her hand rubbing my back makes me nauseated. I think I'm going to be sick.

"I have to get some fresh air," I say.

I stand and almost throw up.

"I have got to get out of here. *Now.*"

❖ ❖ ❖

I awake later with a pounding headache. It's so cold. My mouth feels like someone stuffed it with cottonballs. I hear people arguing with each other. Some guy named Brick is being grilled by a cop over money he (Brick) says he didn't take. A woman yells at the cop, "Leave him alone!"

What is going on? I open my eyes. Diane sits cross-legged on the floor of my apartment watching . . . a soap. Which explains the crime scene. Okay, let's see. Oh, man, I barfed at the Arboretum and Diane drove me home. I remember I also threw up on the landing. I'll never be able to look her in the eye again.

"What soap?" I croak.

Diane kneels by my bed and brushes hair away from my face. "You're awake! How are you feeling?"

"Yucky. Could you get me the blanket out of the closet? I'm freezing."

"I already did. How's your stomach?"

"Okay, I guess."

"I made some chicken soup for you."

I really wish she hadn't mentioned food. I roll out of bed and hobble to the bathroom. Diane follows and holds my hair while I'm sick. I wish she wasn't in here. Doesn't she know this is the one activity that requires the utmost privacy? I try to get up, but I'm too weak. Maybe I'll just rest on the tile floor.

"Muriel, honey, let me help you back to bed, okay?"

"I'll be fine here."

"Put your arm around my shoulder . . . there you go. Now, let's get up. Good. Let me wipe your face with this washcloth. Do you want to brush your teeth?"

"Okay."

I brush and even find the strength to drag a comb through my knotted hair. I catch my reflection in the mirror. If some TV show were casting for a bug-eyed, green-skinned, red-haired Martian, I'd get the role, hands down.

Diane sits on the bed and maneuvers my head onto her lap. She strokes my cheek, which I believe is hypnotizing me into watching the soap. With interest.

After ten minutes of trying to figure out the story, I ask, "Why is that Brick guy in trouble?"

"You really want to know?"

"Uh-huh."

"He raised money to rebuild 9th Street after a fire had devastated the neighborhood. This woman named Gigi actually stole it."

"Who's Gigi?"

"She's Contessa's illegitimate daughter, and she owes this guy named Hector $25,000."

"Oh. Hey, wait a minute. It's Sunday. How come this is on?"

"Honey, remember? You were really sick Sunday. It's Monday."

"Oh, God, I was supposed to be at work!"

"I called in for you."

"But don't you have to work?"

"I called in sick, too."

"Diane?"

"Mmmm?"

"Thank you for taking care of me."

"Sure. Oh, wait, there's Gigi . . . "

I feel very small and safe and protected.

CHAPTER 13

I missed three days of work because of the stomach flu, and it's hard getting back into the swing of things. I can't keep track of which order goes to what table, no matter how many notes I put in the margins of my order pad. I have one more hour to work, then Diane will pick me up at 4:30.

You know, I gotta give her credit. She's been with me since Sunday, checking my temperature, tucking in my blankets, feeding me, and getting me hooked on *The Blinding Light* soap opera. I've never had someone take such good care of me. She's really sweet.

I approach a four top and ask, "Would you like any dessert?"

"That's right, look at the fat woman when you ask that."

"I beg your pardon?"

A woman of sizable, but not unpresentable, bulk asks, "Why is it that you waitresses always look at the fat woman when offering dessert?"

"I'm sorry; I didn't know I was looking at anybody in particular. I didn't mean to offend you. Dessert's on the house."

"Does it look like I need dessert, sweetheart?"

Does she really expect me to answer that?

"Ma'am, I would just like to offer you dessert as an apology."

"Oh, now I'm a 'ma'am'!"

Before she can cause any bodily harm, I interrupt with a smile, "I'll be back in a minute to take your dessert order. If you want any dessert."

That conversation was a waste of my life. I grab the coffee pot to make a round of refills, when I see Allison at the front door. She gestures for me to come over.

"Do you have a few minutes?" she asks.

"Sure." I feel a tingling sensation that hangs between desire and hives.

"I have a proposition for you. I have an apartment above my garage, and my tenant just moved out. I wondered—that woman is waving at you; do you need to go over there?"

The dessert harridan is giving me the international symbol for "Check, please."

"Nah," I say, smiling and waving at the virago. I turn a rapt gaze back to Allison.

"I thought," she continues, "you might be interested in renting it."

What?! A miracle. She likes me so much, she's asking me to live on her property.

"What's the rent?" I ask.

"$375 a month, if you clean the pool twice a week. Sound reasonable?"

"Are you kidding? Totally. I'd love to live at your place. When can I move in?"

"The end of the month?"

"Great!"

"Oh, and it's furnished, so—"

"Excuse me, but I have been waving to you for the last twenty minutes. Could we have our check?"

Warrior Woman stands two inches from my face, and Mexican food does not improve the breath. Or a recovering stomach. I hand her the bill and promptly dismiss her from my consciousness.

"You were saying?"

"Yes, the apartment is furnished, and, of course, I'll include utilities in the rent. Okay?"

"Absolutely okay."

"Great. Well, I have to run. I'm on my way to Paramount. Call me next week?"

Allison's halfway out the door when I realize I haven't asked the most important, make-or-break-the-deal question.

"Wait! Is it on a bus line?"

"A bus line? I don't have a clue. I think there's a bus a few blocks away."

"Great!"

This is fantastic! I am going to live in Beverly Hills, right next to Allison O'Malley, Queen of My Lonely Heart. No more stuck window, no more bus transfers in Hollywood. And a pool! What a deal.

❖   ❖   ❖

"Can you believe it, Jeff? Can you actually believe it?"

I phone from Diane's. I had to call Jeff and tell him the news. Diane is making dinner in the other room.

"It's too cheap to be real," he says.

"Hey, she's a lawyer. Maybe she doesn't need the money."

"I don't know." I detect a note of caution in his voice.

"Come on, Jeff. You're being so weird about this. I get to move out of the tenement!"

"That's true."

"So, can you help me move on the 29th? I only need to take my clothes, TV, and dishes. It'll be one trip, okay?"

"Yeah, that's fine. It's too bad you're at Diane's tonight. Mark's in Santa Barbara visiting his mom, and I hoped we could go out."

"Hey, I have an idea. I'll tell Diane I have to leave early. Can you pick me up here at ten?"

I give him directions, then strategize about how I can tell Diane I am going out with Jeff. What if she's mad? Well, let her be. Jeff's my best friend, and I haven't seen him in practically a week. I cut through the dining room, where the table waits with crystal wine glasses, long ivory candles, and a vase of irises. Pretty.

"Hey, Diane, Jeff just reminded me on the phone that he and I were supposed to go out tonight. I totally forgot. He asked me about two weeks ago, and he'd really be hurt if I let him down. We were supposed to get together at seven o'clock, but I told him I wanted to have dinner with you, so, he's going to pick me up at ten o'clock; is that okay?"

So I bent the truth. Oh, well.

"I was hoping you'd spend the night."

"I know, I'm sorry, but Jeff's counting on this."

Diane turns from checking the rice pilaf on the stove, crosses her arms, and stares at the floor.

"You're mad," I say. "I won't go. I'll call him back right now and—"

"I'm not mad. I'm disappointed, that's all. If you want to go, go. I'm not going to stop you."

"Forget it, I don't have to go."

"No, go."

"Never mind. I'd, um, I'd rather stay here with you."

"You could have fooled me."

"Oh, come on. I do want to be here with you. Here, watch. I'm picking up the phone. I'm dialing Jeff."

Diane turns her back to me and starts basting the chicken.

"Hello, Jeff? Yeah, hi. I can't go tonight. Yeah. We'll go some other time, okay?"

I crumble. I want to spend time with Diane, and I want to go out with Jeff. Why can't I have both?

I walk up behind Diane and embrace her. Her body tenses. I tighten my arms around her and whisper, "I am a low-life scum. Can you forgive me? Please?"

"Of course," she answers. But her body doesn't soften one bit.

Later, in bed, I try to get her to mellow, because her sulking silence at dinner made the whole meal taste like corrugated tin. I pull my fingers through her hair, then kiss her soft shoulder. She has her back to me, so I run my hand to her hip and pull her over. It's like moving a board.

I kiss her forehead, her nose, but when I try for the mouth, she turns away.

"What?" I ask. "What's wrong?"

She shakes her head.

"Are you still mad that I wanted to go out with Jeff? Look, I'm here, aren't I?"

"That's romantic."

"Come on, give me a kiss."

She sits up. "Why don't you just go?"

"What's going on?"

"Why are you really here?"

"I'm here, Diane, because I like you. You make me feel, I don't know, safe. Comforted."

"Mothers can do that, too."

"Not mine."

"I think you're here with me because it's convenient. It's just something to do."

"Please, if I wanted something to do, I'd be with Jeff right now."

Diane stands and furiously throws on her robe; she ties the belt so tight, I'm afraid she'll cut off the circulation to her lower extremities.

"Why do I do this?" she asks. "I'm nice, I make dinner, I open up to people. Why is it that everyone I pick wants to be somewhere else? This is the story of my life."

"Chill out."

"No, I won't. I don't want to do this anymore. Get dressed. Go play with your friend."

"You want too much from me. We're dating; we're not married."

"No shit."

"Okay, fine. I want to have a little fun. I don't need this."

I sling on my T-shirt, then grab my pants from the end of the bed and roughly pull them on. "Where're my boots?"

"In the living room."

"Fine."

I stomp out of the room and out of the house, then practically break my foot as I smack up the kickstand on my bike. Gliding down the darkened sidewalks, I pass by low-slung ranch houses and cement-block apartment complexes. God damn, this city is ugly. After swerving around an old bum wrapped in a gin-soaked blanket, I slide to a stop in front of Jeff's complex. Walking my bike along the narrow path that leads to his tiny, creaking apartment, I mutter every swear word I can think of. Who does Diane think she is? She's so needy for attention. She pisses me off.

As I stand before Jeff's door, I hear the minuscule and obnoxious sound of my conscience working its way into my head.

"You are the problem," it asserts. "Not Diane."

"Oh, really," I answer back. "It's my problem that she's this close to being Sister Sandra of the normal brigade? She's even passive-aggressive. I am not the problem."

"You like her, but don't want to. You're looking for excuses."

"Look, Yoda, I don't need your bullshit."

"I know what you think you want."

"Oh, you do?"

"Be careful what you ask for."

"Shut up," I say out loud. My conscience is full of trite cliches. I ring Jeff's doorbell, then let myself in. Jeff jumps up from his futon couch and turns down the volume on the TV.

"Home Shopping?" I ask.

"Be quiet. I was bored."

"What are you waiting for? Let's go out."

He looks over my shoulder toward the open door. "Is someone with you?"

"No."

"Funny. I thought I heard you talking to someone. Guess you were talking to yourself."

"Talking to—what do you think I am, crazy? Please."

"I guess it was the neighbors."

We stroll down the walkway to the street.

"I don't talk to myself, Jeff."

CHAPTER 14

Jeff and I take my stuff over to Allison's, only to find the driveway blocked by an old woman who bears a striking resemblance to Helmut Kohl.

"Who invited you? What are you doing here?" she shrieks.

We step out of the car, hands visible at our sides. I surreptitiously look around for storm troopers, the SS, or the Beverly Hills Police. We seem to be alone, but one can't be too cautious.

"Um, I'm Muriel? I'm renting the garage apartment?"

The woman scowls at me, her eyes cold and suspicious. "Let me see your driver's license."

"Sure, no problem." I quickly hand it to her.

She looks at it, looks at me, then holds the license to the sun to check for forgeries. As she hands it back, she barks, "Who is he?"

"That's Jeff. He's helping me move."

She stares at him. Apparently, he passes the "Bev Hills test," because her manner becomes more subdued and she steps aside.

"The top of the stairs." She points toward a garage that rivals Norma Desmond's mythical Hollywood estate, with yellow stucco walls and thick plank doors.

Jeff and I don't move until we're sure the woman has goose-stepped her way back into the main house.

"That was bizarre," Jeff murmurs.

"Yeah. I guess I get to deal with a displaced prison guard."

"Who needs an alarm system when you can have her?"

We laugh and head up the stairs to the apartment.

"Way cool, Jeff! Look—French doors! And a deck!"

Jeff walks down the hall. He calls out, "Oh, man! You have a Jacuzzi tub. And check this out—redwood paneling in the bedroom. And a skylight!"

"There's a skylight out here, too."

"Hey, Mutt, a walk-in closet! I would kill for one of these."

"Oh, my God, a stereo TV and a VCR. I have scored!"

I run into the kitchen and meet the soft gleam of brushed chrome countertops and appliances. I couldn't have hoped for a more incredible place. I mean, there's a dishwasher *and* a microwave.

It takes us two trips up the stairs to move my meager belongings. I wave to Jeff from my kitchen window as he drives off to meet Mark for lunch.

I open the French doors to let in some fresh air, then sprawl on the sectional sofa and light a cigarette. It is so quiet. Only the sounds of birds and leaf blowers break this rarefied air. I really can't believe my good fortune.

There's a sharp rap on the door, but before I can get up to answer it, Frau Gestapo bustles in and stands in front of me.

"No smoking in the apartment. If you need to smoke, you may do so on the deck."

"Oh. Sorry." I realize (too late) that there is nowhere to stub out my cigarette, so I walk out on the deck. Frau G. remains in the living room; I hope she can't see me snuff the butt in a planter.

"The key to the pool shed," she announces, setting it with a sharp click on the glass coffee table. "You will find all the equipment you need in there. The instructions are taped to the door."

"Oh, yeah, thanks. I'll get on that first thing in the morning."

"The pool must be cleaned Tuesday and Friday by 11 a.m. I expect you to start today, and have it clean before Miss O'Malley comes home at seven o'clock, yes?"

"Today?"

"It *is* Friday." She pauses briefly, giving me a look that would wilt God, then continues, "There are a few House Rules you should be aware of. One, no guests for more than three days without permission. Two, turn in the rent, to me, on the first of the month, not the second or third. Three, please ask before using the pool. Four, I will pick up the mail and place yours in the box next to your door. Five, you can use the washer and dryer in the main house on Wednesdays between nine o'clock and noon. You agree to these rules, yes?"

"Um, sure."

"Then please sign at the bottom of this page to verify that you understand your responsibilities."

With a trembling hand, I sign my freedom away. The woman picks up the paper and starts toward the door. She turns sharply and says, "I am the housekeeper, Mrs. Schaber. I work here on Mondays, Wednesdays, Fridays, and Saturdays

when necessary. If you have difficulty with anything, please
call me at the main house, yes? Good day."

"Nice meeting you, Mrs. Schaber!" I say to her
retreating figure.

❖   ❖   ❖

Sweeping the pool is harder than I thought, and I've
worked two hours trying to get it right. I wipe at some sweat
threatening to drip from my eyebrow, then sit on a lounge
chair to view my handiwork. Not bad. I mean, it looks clean
enough to me. My back muscles feel really tight. A beer would
help. Good thing I'm meeting Jeff tonight at the bar.

I force myself out of the lounger and put away the
sweeper. As I'm about to lock the shed, I notice Mrs. Schaber
walking slowly along the edge of the pool. Her eyes glued to
the surface of the water, she looks for any microbe that I
might have missed.

"Did I do okay?" I ask.

She holds a finger up to squelch any more comments
I might make, and continues her scrutiny for scum. When
she has finished her perimeter search, she heads over to a
lounge chair, gets on her hands and knees, and appears to be
studying the underside. Whatever.

She stands up, wiping her hands on her apron, and
says, "You haven't scrubbed these down."

"That's part of my job?"

"Anything having to do with the pool is your job.
You also need to sweep and hose the sandstone."

Great. I'm starting to feel like Prissy in *Gone with the
Wind*, downtrodden and enslaved.

"Look, um, I don't mean to cause trouble, but I really
hate to waste water. Wouldn't sweeping be enough?"

"The dust is bad for the lungs."

"Like it matters with this smog?"

She seriously glares at me. I think I'll just do whatever her little heart desires. No need to cause trouble on my first day at Tara.

❖   ❖   ❖

I get cleaned up for my evening out, but can't get the smell of chlorine off my hands. I call for my bus route and learn that I have to walk ten blocks down to Sunset to pick up an east-bound bus. Things aren't as great here as I thought.

I stroll out to the street and fall in line with the nannies, housekeepers, and servants also heading for the bus. They laugh and joke with each other; no one talks to me, but they don't mind my joining their affable, if tired, group.

I'm sweating profusely by the time the bus arrives. These Beverly Hills blocks are long, and the yucko palm trees provide nada shade. I hope I'll dry off in the hour it will take to reach the Rifle. If I miss one of my transfers because of a traffic jam, I'm screwed. Knowing my luck, there'll be a major fatality accident at the corner of Sunset and San Vicente involving a Hummer, a Jetta, and a loose actress.

❖   ❖   ❖

The bus ride went off without a hitch, but I've now waited for Jeff for forty minutes. I've already had a couple beers and feel slightly buzzed and totally pissed. Jesus Christ, the guy has a fucking car; he should be able to meet his best friend on time.

I motion the bartender to bring me another drink, then stand on my toes to try and find Jeff in the crowd. Oh, maybe that's him—nope. I guess I have time to go to the bathroom. I ask the guy next to me to save my seat, promising him a beer when I get back.

No surprise that the line for the women's bathroom is about three hours long. I lean against the wall and stare at my boots, pretending to think about solutions to the Balkan problem. This is my method for avoiding eye contact with anyone, and circumventing the dreaded hive problem. I finally get a stall, only to find there isn't any toilet paper. Damn.

As I head back toward the bar, I run smack into Diane, who, I am very displeased to note, is holding hands with a Melissa wanna-be. You know, shaggy blonde hair, leather jacket.

"Muriel! Hi!" Diane says, beaming. "What a surprise. How are you?"

"Fine," I grunt. "And who's this?"

"Oh, this is my friend Megan. We've known each other forever. Megan, Muriel."

"Nice to meet you," I say. "Well, gotta go. I'm waiting for Jeff."

"Why don't you wait with us?" Megan offers.

Oh, yeah, like I really want to be a third wheel. I walk backwards and say, "Well, I'm sure you two want to be alone. Look, I'll call you—WHOA!"

I trip over a chair, and the next thing I know, I'm flat on my back. Diane and Megan pull me to my feet.

"Are you all right?" Megan asks, a studied look of concern thinly masking hysterical laughter.

"I'm fine." Actually, I'm trying to hide complete and utter humiliation. Diane drags me by the arm into the dreaded back room, and sits me in a booth.

"Don't worry, Jeff can find you back here."

The three of us exchange stares. Well, if truth be told, I'm the only one staring. At the friend. Who's prettier than me. Damn.

"I'm going up to the bar," Diane says. "What do you guys want to drink?"

Megan answers huskily, "Kahlua and coffee."

Kahlua and coffee? What kind of drink is that? Please! The only thing that should go into coffee is half-and-half. I request my standard suds.

Diane leaves us alone. I look at Megan. She looks back. I dig out a Marlboro; she digs out an organic American Spirit. I fumble for my matchbook; she deftly pulls out a silver butane lighter.

"Need a light?" she drawls.

"Thanks. So, Megan, how long have you known Diane?"

"Forever. We grew up next door to each other."

"Really?"

"Yeah."

She flicks her ash on the floor, flips her hair over her shoulder, and looks for Diane. I flick my ash in the ashtray, flip my hair over my shoulder, and look for Jeff. Desperately. We don't say another word until Diane comes back with the drinks.

Diane chirps, "Megan just got back from South America."

"I'm an anthro."

"As in anthropologist?" I ask.

"Yep."

"Wow. South America," I say. "You know, I was an anthropology major. I didn't realize it actually led to a *job* in anthropology."

"All you need are a few connections. And a Ph.D."

Diane says, "Megan breezes in and out of town, always on her way to the edge of the planet. It's very romantic."

"It's not that romantic." Megan grins and puts her arm around Diane's shoulders.

I want to toss this "anthro" into a tar pit. I'm a little upset that Diane has thrown me over for someone better-looking with a better job. Not that I want to be with Diane or anything. Although I feel a tad jealous at the moment. How do I exit this scene gracefully?

"Shit!" Megan yells as I "accidentally" knock over my beer bottle.

"Oh, I'm so sorry, Megan," I say. "Did it get on your lap?"

"I'm fine. I'm fine. I just need to go to the restroom to clean up." She plants a kiss on Diane's lips. "I'll be back."

She saunters off, wiping the front of her jeans. I look sheepishly at Diane and say, "I am so embarrassed about that. I'm such a klutz."

Diane glares at me and hisses, "You are such an asshole."

My mouth opens to retort, but I really don't have an answer for that comment. Diane slams out of her seat and heads toward the bathroom.

"Diane, wait, I didn't mean to . . . "

Ah, crap.

❖   ❖   ❖

"Sorry, Mutt, I had to work late and I didn't know your new phone number."

"Hey, no problem. It gave me plenty of time to entirely screw up my life."

Jeff and I sit at the bar in the boys' room, trying to hide from Margaret Mead.

"What did you do this time?" he asks.

"Nothing."

"Nothing?"

"Okay, Diane strolled in here with some chick, hand in hand, no less, and I accidentally knocked my beer into the girl's lap. She's probably going to kill me, and if she doesn't, Diane will."

Jeff unsuccessfully stifles a laugh. "That's mature."

"I couldn't help it. She deserved it. She had her hands all over Diane. And get this: she has a Ph.D. in anthropology. It was making me sick."

"Since when do you care who Diane sees?"

"Of course I care, Jeff. People get jealous of their ex-girlfriends, you know."

"You slept with her, what, two or three times?"

"Yeah, so?"

"You have no right to be jealous. You couldn't give a shit about Diane. All you ever talk about lately is Allison, Allison, Allison."

"Did I say anything about Allison? My feelings toward Allison have nothing to do with my relationship with Diane. And don't roll your eyes at me!"

"Mutt, why don't you grow up?"

"Why are you mad at me? I didn't do anything to you."

"Don't you get it, Mutt? Diane is sweet and loving and, until recently, available. But you'd rather be Allison's live-in pool cleaner."

"That's ridiculous!"

"Allison is never, ever, going to be interested in you. So get over her."

"You don't know anything about it. She likes me. I know she does."

"We used to have real conversations. Now it's all about you and your fucked-up love affairs. Or should I say non-affairs." Jeff shakes his head, then continues, "Mark was right. You are so self-centered."

"Mark said that? I can't believe it." God, Mark hates me that much? Jeff agrees with him? What the hell is going on?

"I want to go home, Jeff."

"Right now?"

"I can't believe you think I am self-centered. Jesus."

"I'm sorry I said anything."

"No, you're not. You said that to deliberately hurt me."

"Come on!"

"Give me a ride home."

"It's forty minutes out of my way!"

"The bus takes over an hour."

"It's your own fault for moving to Beverly Hills."

"Jeff, you just totally insulted me; now you won't take me home?"

"This is exactly what I mean."

"Jeff, goddamn it—"

"Okay, okay. Let's go."

"Thank you for your generosity of spirit," I respond sarcastically.

"Knock it off."

We manage to maintain a polite silence the entire ride home. I feel like I've been slapped over and over again. When he pulls in the driveway, I make no attempt to exit the car.

"Aren't you getting out?" he asks.

"Turn off the engine, Jeff. Turn it off. Thank you. I've figured out what's going on here."

"Nothing's going on, Mutt. We had a fight."

"No, there's a lot going on. I think Mark is trying to turn you against me."

"What?"

"No, listen. Mark wants you to move to Chicago, right? So, he decides in his wicked little head that the only way you will go is if you have nothing to keep you here. So he poisons you against me, and he wins. It's quite a clever plot. Can't you see the demented way your boyfriend thinks?"

Jeff looks out his window. He chews on his bottom lip and runs his hand through his hair. "We are moving to Chicago. Next month."

"I knew it."

"Mark is not trying to 'poison me' against you."

"Yes, he is."

"Mutt, grow up."

"Go to hell." I get out of the car and slam the door. I don't even look back as Jeff drives away.

I walk up the stairs, anger building with each step. I enter my spotless and utterly lonely living room. I turn on the track lights, which highlight a gargantuan bouquet of tropical flowers sitting on my coffee table. I open the card, which reads, "Welcome to your new home. Allison."

"See, Jeff," I say to the walls, "I told you she liked me."

CHAPTER 15

It's been a week of complete misery. Jeff and I don't talk at work, Diane won't return my calls, and I have yet to see Allison. I can't concentrate on the videos I rented, even though I've hooked the TV up to the speakers for maximum viewing enjoyment.

Friday rolls around again, and I have zero plans for the weekend. Well, at least I have a new "girl gumshoe" book to read. I pop down to the main house to get permission to use the pool. So far, I've been successful at avoiding Mrs. Schaber, except at white-glove inspection time. But if I want to swim, I'll have to bite the bullet and pray that the commandant's in a generous mood.

Mrs. Schaber presides over a kitchen filled with busy buzzing worker bees.

Without looking at me, she asks, "Do you have a problem?"

"No, no. I would like to use the pool."

She waves at a tuxedo-clad woman who is holding a box of wine glasses. "You know where to set up the bar! Here, come with me."

I guess she didn't hear me, so I follow them into the living room. Mrs. Schaber gives the woman a fifteen-minute lecture on how to properly stack the glasses, which I believe has left the young woman on the verge of hysteria or suicide.

"You're still here?" Mrs. Schaber asks me.

"Um, I want to know if I can use the pool."

"Are you out of your mind? Can't you see I'm busy?"

"What does that have to do with—"

"Where are your shoes? You're tracking dirt all over the house."

"I'm sorry." I check the bottom of each foot. Seems pretty clean to me. "Anyway, could I please—"

"No. Can't you see we are setting up a party?"

"Yeah, but I won't—"

"No. Tomorrow, perhaps."

"Okay." My attempt at fun foiled, I head towards the front door.

"Use the kitchen door."

"Okay, sorry." Who said the feudal system was dead?

The front door opens. "Ah, excellent," Allison exclaims. "The house looks wonderful, Mrs. Schaber."

I stop in my tracks. "Hi," I say. Jeez, I've missed her.

"Oh, Muriel. Are you helping with the party?"

"Um, no. I just came to see if I could swim, but Mrs.—"

"Yes, of course. Why would you have to ask?" Allison says, surprised.

Pointing at Mrs. Schaber, I say, "But she told—"

"Of course you can use the pool," Mrs. Schaber interrupts sharply. "Just be out by seven o'clock."

"But you said—"

"You must have misunderstood."

"But you—"

Allison starts up the stairs, then calls out, "Muriel, why don't you come tonight? Eight-ish? It's just a few friends and business associates. I'd love for you to join us." Her voice evaporates as she reaches the upstairs landing.

I look at Mrs. Schaber, fully expecting a recant of the pool permission.

"Well, go swim," she growls.

❖   ❖   ❖

Through my kitchen window, I watch some of the guests arrive, then wait a half hour before making my appearance. I want to slip easily into the crowd; this technique will save me from having to talk to anybody one-on-one. When I walk through the front door, I am greeted by . . . no one. What's up? I hear muffled voices coming from the dining room. Okay, so the finger food must be in there. Great, I'm hungry.

I swing into the room and am confronted by swiveling heads and abrupt silence. Oh, shit. It's a Sit-Down Dinner. And, double shit, Diane's one of the guests.

"Um, hi," I stutter. "Sorry I'm late."

Allison says smoothly, "It's not a problem. I kept a place for you. I'm so glad you could make it."

I sit down and Allison continues with introductions.

"Everyone, this is my very dear tenant, Mutt, or rather, Muriel. Mutt's her nickname. I think you know Diane, and I'd like you to meet . . ."

These people could be wearing name tags, and I'd still not remember them. I divide my consciousness between Diane's obvious hostility and Allison's gracious acceptance of my faux pas. Conversation slowly starts up. I force myself to make small talk, smile at every insipid joke, and manage, every so often, to sneak a peek at Allison.

When dinner ends (thankfully, as the food ranked high in drabness), the group meanders into the living room for coffee and an after-dinner drink. I stop Allison on her way to join the guests.

"Allison, I'm sorry."

"Not to worry. You didn't know."

"I swear I would have been on time."

"Mutt, it's all right. Let's go join the others."

I try to pay attention to what everyone is saying, half understanding and less than half interested in their Hollywood jargon. Diane pointedly ignores me. Every time I try to approach her, she turns toward another guest and becomes totally immersed in a conversation. Since I seem to be a noncontributing member of this fête, I excuse myself, pretending to head toward the bathroom, but instead making a sharp detour through the kitchen to my apartment.

At home, I grab a beer and sprawl on a steamer chair on the deck. I bet no one even notices I've left. That's me, the invisible underdog. The Mutt. I've gotta do something about my miserable state, but what?

"Knock knock."

Framed by the French doors, her hair highlighted from behind like an angel in a Renaissance fresco, stands Diane.

"You left the party," she remarks.

"How come you didn't return any of my calls, Diane?"

She shrugs and answers simply, "I was angry."

"No kidding. Like that wasn't obvious tonight."

"Well . . ."

"It certainly surprised me to see you here. I didn't know you and Allison had become bosom buddies."

"She wanted me to meet an agent. Teddy Donato?"

"Whoever. You want a beer?"

"No thanks."

I escape to the kitchen, hoping Diane will disappear in the meantime. She drives me crazy. I can't help it—I am not denying I'm attracted to her. But, well, there's Allison. When I return, Diane is leaning against the deck railing, gazing at the night sky.

Without turning towards me, she says, "Megan and I are friends. That's all."

"It's not my business. You do what you want."

"You sure made it your business at the bar."

"If you're just friends, how come she kissed you on the lips?"

"To get back at you for your rude and transparent behavior."

"Transparent?"

"Muriel, people can read you like a book," she says. "Everything you feel shows up immediately on your face."

"Oh, really?" I put on a poker face and ask in my best Mr. Spock monotone, "What am I feeling now?"

"You feel lonely and out of place."

"Hah! That's not true at all. I feel totally great. I have a perfect house. I have it made. I just couldn't stand to listen to the drivel in there anymore. I left. So there."

"Really."

I pace and say, "Okay, okay, so I felt uncomfortable at the party. Big deal. It doesn't matter, anyway."

"What does matter to you, Muriel?"

"What matters? A lot matters to me! But you should—you should see that in my face, right?"

I find my cigs and rip the box trying to get one out. I light it and take a deep, long drag.

"I wish you wouldn't do that."

"Why not? It's my deck; I can smoke if I want."

"No, I wish you'd stop pacing. You're making me dizzy."

I sit with a thud on the steamer chair.

"Are you in love with Allison?" she asks.

"What?" I sputter. "Don't be ridiculous!"

"I have eyes, Muriel. And I'm not stupid. You spent most of dinner staring at her. Everyone noticed."

"I did not!"

Diane sighs. "I don't want to argue with you. You know, what you did to Megan was really childish. But, hey, it made me think you actually cared about me. In some weird way. I don't know."

"Diane, I'm sorry I pissed you off. Megan was just so possessive of you, and . . ."

I fall silent, the width of the three-car garage below now a giant chasm between us.

Finally, Diane clears her throat and says, "I really care for you, Muriel."

"Oh, man. I want to be your friend, I do, but—"

"Great, I'm getting the brush-off."

"No, no, you're not, it's just that . . . I don't know." How can I explain my conflicting emotions to her?

"I was furious tonight when I saw how you looked at Allison. I wanted you to look at me like that."

"Did she look at me?"

"Did you really just ask me that?"

"Well, I—"

"Look," she says briskly, "Figure out your thing with Allison."

She makes a wide berth around me and goes out the front door. I run down the stairs after her.

"Diane! Wait! Why can't we be friends? I feel like I'm losing all my friends."

"Maybe you should try a little harder at being nice.
And honest."

"Wait!"

She's gone. I've driven her away. Why do I keep
blowing it with people?

CHAPTER 16

The only thing in life you can count on is that there will never be enough money left at the end of the month. Hey, I'll be honest. Sometimes, when that fourth week rolls around, I smoke generic-brand cigarettes. I put them in a Marlboro box just to look good. But counting on people? No way. Friends are transitory, lovers are mercurial, and fantasies are ephemeral.

Yet, in this great sprawling city there's, like, three-point-five million people, of whom at least 10,000 might be viable candidates for new friends. That means I could find a potential buddy on every corner. Well, maybe just on certain corners. So what do I have to be depressed about?

Okay, Jeff's moving, and even though he'll have every intention of staying in touch with me, I know he'll drop off the face of the earth. And Diane's been a good friend—a great friend—but she made it pretty clear last night that she wants nothing to do with me. Allison? Well, we'll see.

I've been doing some hard thinking about the Diane situation. I've got it all figured, similar to how I sorted out Jeff's antagonistic behavior. Diane seemed to be nuts about me and did a lot of favors for me (including, but not limited to, vomit cleanups). Boy. But what have I given her? Nothing.

I got something; she got nothing. Bad deal, plain and simple. I understand her reason for walking out on me.

The fact of the matter is, you've got to learn from your past mistakes. I never did anything to deserve Diane's affection. And this has made it very clear to me that there should be give-and-take in a relationship. So I've decided to work on giving more. I'm just not quite sure how to do it, though.

I suit up and head for the pool, checking the temperature on the thermometer by my door. Whoa—71 degrees. No wonder I have goose bumps. At least the pool will be warm. The sky is not its normal urine yellow, but is tinged with lumpy gray clouds. Good, maybe it'll rain and clear out the smog for a couple hours. I love the air after a rain. It smells so fresh. Unfortunately, without the smog, it's too bright, and the glare gives me a bad headache. I guess there's a trade-off for everything.

I round the corner to the patio and see I am not the only one who yearned for a Saturday morning swim. Lucky me. Allison backstrokes across the water. Wow, she could be a championship swimmer, her stroke is so powerful. I wish I could swim like that. The dog paddle is my preferred water mode. Allison waves to me, then swims over to where I'm standing.

"Good morning! Come in, the water's fantastic."

I sit on the pool edge, the sandstone cutting sharply into the backs of my thighs. Dangling my feet in the water, allowing them time to acclimate, I wrap a towel around my shoulders to keep out the chill.

Allison buoys herself up with an arm along the pool edge and asks, "What happened to you last night?"

Oh my God, she actually noticed my departure.

"What do you mean?" I respond. "Oh, I was just tired, so I went home."

"We wondered where you disappeared to. We missed you."

"You did?"

"Of course. God, what a boring crowd."

"Even Diane?"

"No. No. I mean, Diane's your friend, right? She wasn't boring at all."

"Why do you have parties if you're bored with everyone who comes to them?"

"I don't—do I think everyone is boring?" She says this as a rhetorical question. "No. That's an exaggeration. They're simply business acquaintances." She frowns slightly. "It's not like they're my friends."

"I would only have parties with friends. Then you can't be bored."

"You're a much smarter person than I am."

"Oh, no, that's not true. I wasn't implying anything like that."

Allison looks up at the heavy sky, then back at me. "Why don't you swim before it starts to rain?"

"I will. I have to do this in increments. Hey, I'm up to my waist now. I'll be in soon."

Diving directly in the water would send my body into shock. As a little girl, my mother used to force me into the water before I was ready for the cold.

"Come on, honey," she said silkily. "Don't be a baby. Everything's going to be just fine."

"It's too cold, Mommy."

"Honey, if it's too cold, why are so many people in the water? Look, Sandra's already swimming. Why can't you be more like her?"

I hugged my arms tight across my chest, both for modesty and for body heat, and prayed for my mother to schlep her humongous body into the locker room and leave me in peace.

"Mommy, why can't I sit on the steps? I want to sit on the steps."

"Honey," she stated, that silky voice hard as cast iron, "ONLY BABIES SIT ON THE STEPS."

I squatted near the edge and swirled my finger or toe in the water, hoping my mother would take it as a sign of my imminent immersion. Then, just when I thought I had her fooled, she stepped forward and shoved me into the icy depths. As I sputtered for breath, her maniacal laughter pierced my eardrums and rattled inside my very angry little head. I never hated her more. It was the same script from age five to fifteen, and I never once saw it coming.

So now I relish having the freedom to take twenty minutes to adjust to water temp. No more involuntary baptisms.

I slide up to my neck, then begin a slow sidestroke.

"Deep thoughts?"

"Hmm?"

I'm bewildered to see Allison toweling off by a lounge chair. Wasn't she just in the water? Her body looks vulnerable, thin in the way of people who work too long and forget to eat. Thin in the way of someone who's lonely.

"Oh, I just felt a drop of rain," she says. "As if we need another downpour this year. Why don't you have a cappuccino with me? Come by when you've changed."

I nod, then swim around a little, luxuriating in the weightlessness of my body.

You know, that wasn't exactly right, saying I hated my mother most when she flung me into the pool.

I hated her most when she died.

❖   ❖   ❖

The rain falls full force, and I'm afraid it's going to pummel the miniature roses I cut from the garden. I cover the small bouquet with the edge of my jean jacket and charge across the patio to Allison's.

I find her in the kitchen, measuring out espresso. I walk up behind her and present the flowers. Even in sweats and wet hair, she looks drop-dead gorgeous.

"These are lovely. There's a vase on the shelf above the pantry. Could you take care of them? I'm trying to remember how this machine works."

I get the vase, pour the water, and shove in the roses. No matter which way I place a stem, it ends up flopped over the vase edge, pretending to be dead. Someday, I'll have to learn the art of flower arrangement.

"There," she says, "got it working. I can't believe how much rain we've had this year, can you?"

"Um, no, not really."

Allison begins to steam the milk, and the machine starts grunting like an angry pig. I hope I don't lose my hearing from the intense decibel level.

"How do you like the apartment?" she says over the squealing.

"It's great. I sure appreciate that you're letting me rent it."

"I'm sorry, what?" She gestures helplessly towards the machine.

"It's great! Thanks."

"I can't hear you. Let me finish the milk."

We walk out to the living room, cappuccinos in hand, and Allison sits on the floor in front of the coffee table. I opt for the comfort of the black leather sofa.

"What I was saying earlier was that I'm really happy to be living here."

"Good. Good. So, everything's working out?"

"Yeah, fine. Great."

"I love this part of town," she says. "It's so quiet, don't you think?"

"It's really nice."

Allison checks her watch, then glances out the front window.

"Are you waiting for someone?" I ask.

"No, I'm sorry, I zoned out for a minute. I've been so swamped at work lately, and I haven't been able to sleep, so . . . Well, it's five o'clock somewhere in the world. How about a brandy?"

"No thanks."

"Just to take the chill out of the day?"

She opens a crystal decanter and pours the amber liquid into two glasses. I feel like I've stepped onto the set of a Nick and Nora movie.

"I didn't know people actually used decanters," I say. "I thought it was only a film thing."

"It's so 1930s, isn't it?"

I take a glass from her and say, "Yeah, I know, work's tough, isn't it? Sometimes I get so wiped out at the end of the day, I can barely walk."

"Do you? Waitressing? Is it really that stressful?"

"Oh, man, you wouldn't believe it. I mean, you have people yakking at you all day, wanting impossible things. Nobody's ever satisfied, and you get yelled at for whatever's wrong, even if it's not your fault. You screw up an order, and boom—no tip. Stop laughing, I'm serious! The tension is incredible. And to top it off, I waitress in my dreams. The job never lets go of me."

Allison bursts into hysterical laughter and snorts. She immediately covers her nose and forces herself to be serious.

"Oh, my God, Allison, you snorted!"

"No, I didn't."

"You did. That was way too funny."

She downs her brandy, then gets up and walks toward the kitchen. "I did not snort. I do not snort."

I hop up and tag along. "You did."

"I didn't."

"Yes, you did!"

"No. Yes. All right, I snorted," she says huffily. "Do we have to keep talking about it?"

"It just makes you more lovable."

She stops midway through the living room and turns to me with a quizzical look. "More lovable?"

Uh-oh. Did I just say that? Really not cool.

"Did I say lovable? I meant, it's—cute—you know?"

"Mutt, if there's one thing I've never been, it's cute. I hate cute."

"Okay, um, it's adorable."

"That's a subset of cute."

"It's charming? In a quaint sort of way?"

"Mmm-hmm?"

"Should I try to extract my foot from my mouth? Or should I just shut up?"

Allison sighs deeply and remarks, "You don't have to do either. I was embarrassed; that's all."

"All right. How's this?" I ask, hoping to salvage the situation. "You are not cute, you're definitely not adorable, and you are certainly not the least bit charming."

"Thank you. You are, however, all three."

I freeze up, then my heart takes a few jumps inside my chest.

Allison sits in a window seat overlooking the pool. "Maybe we do have similar jobs. We both deal with pains-in-the-asses. Some days, I can't stand my job."

"Like I can? At least you get paid a lot of money to be miserable."

"That's true. But it doesn't mean anything. Money isn't the be-all and end-all of life."

"It's pretty close."

"No, really. Can money buy you friends?"

"Um, yes," I respond.

"Can it buy you love?"

"I believe it can sometimes."

"Can it buy you happiness?"

"Most definitely."

"Come on," she replies. "You're not serious."

"Well, to be perfectly frank, only people with money have the luxury to ask those questions. People like me tend to think of money as a very good thing. Like, if I had money, it would change my life. I could buy a car, and I wouldn't have to rely on public transportation. I could go where I want, when I want. Which, you see, equals freedom. Which equals happiness."

"A car would make you happy?"

"Absolutely."

"Then it's done. That Blazer sitting in the garage? It's yours to borrow while you're here." With utmost solemnity she adds, "I have now bestowed happiness upon you."

I'm stunned. I know I'm looking at Allison with an attractively slack jaw, but anyone would in this situation.

"Wow, Allison, I . . . that's a really generous offer, but I couldn't accept it. Thanks, though."

"Why not? I'm not using it. Cars are meant to be driven. So drive it."

"No, I can't. Really. It feels too much like charity."

"Charity? Don't be silly. Look, take the car, and every so often you can run errands for me. That's not charity. Actually, it would really help me out."

"Well—"

"Just take the car."

"I don't know. It doesn't feel right."

"Mutt, see it as a business deal. I get something and you get something, okay? I won't take no for an answer."

How can I turn down an offer of wheels? I could come and go anytime I pleased. No more putting up with the druggies who hang out at my bus transfer points. And, in exchange, I'll do a few errands. No problem.

"What the hell," I say. "It's a deal. Let's shake on it."

As our hands meet, I ask, "Did you, you know, mean what you said earlier?"

"About what?"

"You know, about me being 'cute' and all."

"Oh, that. Of course."

I let out the breath I've been holding. "Wow. That's nice."

I look into Allison's hazel eyes and smile. She slowly smiles back, then looks down at our enclasped hands.

"Would you mind," she says softly, "telling me why I find you so appealing?"

"Could it be my girl-next-door appeal?"

"Mmm." She shakes her head slowly. "You remind me of what it's like to be free."

I look at her face; I think she's gonna cry, because her mouth is tight at the corners. I reach up and pull her close to me. She grabs me tightly with both arms and buries her head in my neck.

A knock at the door makes her move away sharply, and she wipes her eyes quickly with the back of her hand.

"God, who wants something, now?" Allison opens the door to a woman with power hair and just a touch too much makeup, which isn't doing a good job of covering the sharpness of her features.

"Kay," Allison says, putting a hand on her hips.

"You can't ignore me."

"I can do anything I want."

"God damn it, Allie." Allison opens the door wide enough for Kay to see me. "I didn't know you had company."

Allison turns toward me. "Give us a few minutes?"

"Sure."

She smiles. "I'll call you later tonight, okay?"

As I exit through the kitchen, I have an urge to hide in the pantry and eavesdrop. Kay must be her ex. What a bitch; I hate her already. I'm sure she's the one making Allison so sad. I bolt through the back door when I hear them coming.

❖   ❖   ❖

Peeking over the top of my deck, I check to see if the white BMW has left yet. Damn. She's been down there three hours. What can they have to talk about? I squat down and take a quick drag, then wave the smoke away with my arm, so no one will know I'm spying.

CHAPTER 17

I pick up Allison's dry cleaning, then swing by the florist and buy a beautiful arrangement of white lilies. I plan to leave them on her porch, so that when she comes home from work tonight, she'll know someone has thought of her.

This morning, the slam of a car door jolted me from my sleep. And it was a pissed-off slam. The flowers will cheer Allison up.

CHAPTER 18

Jeff hasn't shown for work. Needless to say, I have had the sole responsibility of cleaning and setting the tables, and filling every fucking salt and pepper shaker on the planet. I don't have the patience for anything as Zen as pepper pouring.

Customers come in like flies; every time the door opens, I look up, hoping it's Jeff. No sign. I'm getting worried. What if he's had a car accident? What if he's in the hospital? I run to the manager's office.

"Hey, could you call Jeff's house? I'm scared that something might have happened to him."

The manager nods and I head back to my tables. Jesus Christ, when did all these people get here? How in the hell can I serve them all? I take a deep breath. I'll have to convince everyone to eat fajitas and drink margaritas; that's the only way I can survive this juggernaut. If someone orders something deviant like iced tea or a dinner salad, I'll be sunk. Juan breezes past me at the speed of the proposed L.A./Vegas supertrain. Damn, he's efficient. There's already water and chips on thirteen tables. What a joke. All right, Mutt, take it one table at a time.

"Excuse me," someone says from the table behind me. I keep my eyes focused on the five businessmen at Table 1, who are spewing out complicated orders involving tostadas with no shells and extra cream for their coffee.

The moron behind me taps my hip, which really irks me. I turn on him, a Stepford smile masking my frustration. "I'm sorry, but you are Table 10. I am on Table 1 and I am the only waiter in the entire restaurant. You will have to wait your turn, like everyone else, okay? Great."

I don't wait for a response, but slide over to Table 2. Around the time I hit Table 5 (figuratively, not literally), I catch Jeff out of the corner of my eye. He's calmly taking orders on the other side of the room. I feel like simultaneously kissing his feet and slapping his face.

We reach the kitchen at the same time and throw our orders at the cooks.

"Where the fuck were you?" I ask.

"Mark drove me. He was running late. Sorry."

"I had to set up the whole restaurant by myself."

"I said I was sorry."

"Did you expect me to take all those orders alone?"

"Get off my ass, Mutt. Everything's covered now, okay?"

"I can't believe you are so fucking late. I thought you were in a fucking accident. I thought you'd died. You piss me off, Jeff."

"I piss you off?! I could have been dead on the side of the road, and I piss you off?!"

I head out to the dining room, three plates of sizzling fajitas balanced on one arm. "You're not dead, so I have every right to be pissed off."

After finishing off the motley lunch bunch, I settle down on a bar stool. A few stragglers remain, and Jeff and I take our time serving them.

Then, just when I think the rest of my shift will flow smoothly by, SHE walks in. You know who I mean. The jet-setting, bed-hopping anthro from hell. Damn, I thought she was supposed to be in Antarctica or somewhere. She saunters over to a table and makes a point of turning her chair so she can stare at me. She lights a cigarette, flips her hair, and assaults me with a shit-eating grin. No doubt she's meeting Diane.

I lean over to Jeff and say under my breath, "Take Table 3."

Jeff looks over at Megan, then goes back to counting his tips. "Why?"

"Because I asked! Jeff, this is a crisis and an emergency. Please take the table."

Jeff slowly looks over at her again, carefully folds his money, and puts it in his pocket. "No."

"Oh, come on, why not?"

"Why should I?"

"Because I asked, Jeff. Because you're my friend and you wouldn't want me to get hurt."

"It's your section. You take the table."

"What the hell is with you? Do you know who that is?"

"I don't have a clue, and I don't care."

"That's—that's her. You know!"

"Please don't tell me she's yet another crush," he drawls sarcastically.

"Jeff, take the fucking table. You were late. You owe it to me."

"No."

"No? Jeff, that's the woman I spilled the beer on. She's probably meeting Diane, who I am not on very good terms with. But you wouldn't know that, because you've been ignoring me for the past twenty years."

"Diane came to her senses and broke up with you?"

"Oh, Jesus," I say. "What does it matter? Just go serve her."

Jeff rubs his chin and thoughtfully looks me up and down. "Apologize to me."

"What? Apologize? Okay, I'm sorry I was an asshole earlier. I shouldn't have yelled at you. You worried me; I'm glad you're not dead. I am sorry, sorry, sorry."

"You mean it?"

"Absolutely, totally, and utterly. Okay?"

"Thank you."

"You're welcome," I say, breathing a sigh of relief. Jeff begins to recount his money, stacking rows of shiny quarters on the bar in front of him.

"I apologized, Jeff. Aren't you going to take the table?"

"No. But I accept your apology."

I glare at him. Does he understand that forcing me to wait on Megan is tantamount to making me walk the plank? Obviously, he doesn't understand the seriousness of this situation.

"Jeff, I apologized under the assump—"

"Which of you has Section 1?"

Unbeknownst to me, the manager has made a rare appearance in the dining area. I turn to him sheepishly and say, "Me."

"The customer at Table 3 is waiting."

"Sorry, I didn't see her," I humbly mutter as I plod my way to my doom.

Have you ever noticed that, when you face a thing you don't want to face, it becomes twenty feet tall? I'm serious. I watch Megan grow to the size of a Macy's Thanksgiving Day Parade float. Her hugeness casts a dank shadow over me. The glow from her American Spirit cig equals the size of the Malibu fire. Her hair rivals the Great Plains. Compared to her, I'm a Chihuahua. No, they're too vicious. I'm a Yorkshire terrier. And the runt of the litter to boot. This sucks.

"Sit down." The venom of her command hits me in the face like scalding, desert wind.

"Hi," I squeak in a voice that would make a hamster proud. I shake my head and rub my eyes. The Chimera has become life-sized again. Thank God.

"Would you sit down?" Megan asks.

I slide into a seat across from her.

"I don't like you very much," she says. "But Diane does. Don't ask me why."

"Right now, she doesn't like me too much."

She leans forward and sets her elbows so hard on the table, the salsa bowl jumps two inches to the right.

"Look, Murlene—"

"Muriel."

"Muriel. Diane's my friend; I don't like to see my friends hurt. For some reason, she's taken it into her head that you are the one she wants."

"Why are you telling me this?"

"Because I want you to stay the hell away from her."

"You can't tell me what to do."

"I can and I just did."

"This is ridiculous. It's none of your business what Diane and I do. What if I told you that I'm crazy about her?"

"You're not. That's my problem with you."

"I don't have to listen to this shit."

"Leave her alone, all right?"

I push back the chair and stand above her. "What can I get you?"

"Just leave her alone."

"Look, I'll get another waiter to take your order, because I really don't appreciate people interfering with my life."

Megan stubs out her cigarette, carefully places her lighter in her purse, then tips over her water glass. I jump back, but not in time to avoid a splash that lands directly on my crotch. I'm gonna kill this bitch.

"You know," I steam, "just for that, I'll be calling Diane real soon."

I put my hands in front of me, hoping to cover the embarrassing spot, and march over to Jeff. "I hope you're happy with yourself."

He chuckles, then says, "Never felt better."

CHAPTER 19

I jog the Blazer down to 3rd to get a car wash, mainly to circumvent the stop-and-stop traffic on Sunset. I barely even notice the car is finished until the attendant swings his rags three inches from my face and swears at me in Spanish. I drive off the lot and head back up La Cienega. What is going on with Jeff, lately? I can't believe he let me fall into the clutches of Megan. I need a smoke. I reach over to my backpack, only to find an empty seat. I check the back, trying not to swerve too far into the other lane. Not there. Oh, man. Don't tell me I left it at the Stars and Suds. By the time I get back there, the only thing left will be the shoulder straps. I pull a U-turn across a double yellow line. I'm not stupid. I check for cops before I make the move. I mean, in this town, assault is a misdemeanor, but a traffic violation is a federal offense. You learn to watch your back.

I swing into the auto wash and run inside. Where is it? A better question would be, who stole it? I check around the indoor seating. No luck. Did I leave it outside? Did I sit outside? I don't remember. I open the door and plow right into Diane. Oh, no. I can't deal with this. I've got to find my backpack.

"Muriel!"

"Um, stay right there, I gotta find my backpack."

I do a search over, under, and around the patio seats. Oh, man. Allison's gas card was in my wallet. Where else could it be?

"Muriel?" Diane calls out.

"Just give me a second."

"But, Muriel—"

"Just a minute!"

"Fine. Here's your backpack. The cashier had it."

After she thrusts it at me, I quickly scan the contents. I'm in luck. Nothing's missing. Now I can deal with Diane. She's standing beside a pinball machine that has an "Out of Order" sign taped to its pockmarked surface.

"I'm sorry. I panicked. Thanks for helping."

She doesn't answer.

"How'd you know it was my backpack?"

"I saw you getting into your car. The attendant ran after you, but you didn't turn around."

"I had a visit from Megan."

"What?" She sighs and says to herself, "Why did she do that?"

"She's kinda scary."

"Not really."

We walk outside and are surrounded on all sides by the clamor of traffic squealing across wet cement. Diane is so pretty, such a clean image against the saffron sky. I remember making love; how she made me feel warm and sheltered.

"I—" She stops herself, and looks away.

"How have you been?"

"All right, I guess. And you?"

"I'm fine. Fine."

"Good."

I miss her. I miss her steadiness.

"Diane, please, can't we—"

"My car's ready. I'll see you around, Muriel."

I watch her walk away from me. Why couldn't I just be nice? I catch up with her as she's climbing in her Jeep.

"Can I call you?" I ask.

"That'd be . . . Don't bother."

"Diane, don't drive away from me. Wait! We need to—" I'm interrupted by the screech of her tires as she pulls onto the street.

Oh, Diane.

❖   ❖   ❖

When I get home, I tap lightly on Allison's door. No answer. I knock more loudly, then put my ear up to the door. Definitely someone in there. The door swings open before I can step back, so I probably look a bit foolish.

"Oh, hi, Allison. I was just, um, trying to see if— never mind. Hey, I thought I'd bring you this book to read. It's my favorite Virginia Woolf."

"Thank you," she says, taking the book. "I don't have much time to read, but—"

"I thought you might enjoy it. Oh, did you get your dry cleaning? I gave it to Mrs. Schaber."

"I did. Thanks for picking it up."

"Well, that's all I had to—No, wait." I take a deep breath. "I wonder if you'd like to come over to my place sometime. I'd like to fix you dinner. If that's all right."

"That sounds lovely."

"Saturday night?"

She laughs lightly and says, "I'll check my schedule and get back to you."

"Okay. Well, thanks again."

"Sure."

I turn toward my apartment, but Allison places a hand on my arm to stop me.

"Wait, Mutt. Do you happen to know if there's been a funeral in the neighborhood recently?"

"A funeral?" I ask, confused.

"Yes. Some flowers were delivered here by mistake."

"How do you know they were for a funeral?"

"They were white lilies. What else could they have been for?"

"Really?! Lilies are funeral flowers? What do you know? Oh. Hey, now that I think about it, I saw a procession a couple of days ago."

"Hmmm. Anyway, I'll get back to you about Saturday. Unless . . . are you free tonight?"

"Um, yeah. Of course."

"How about a drive?"

"Okay. Sure. That'd be . . . that'd be great."

"Come by around nine, okay? Do you happen to know who died?"

"What?"

"The funeral? I'd like to forward the flowers."

"Oh, the funeral. I don't have a clue."

"Oh, well. See you tonight."

I stomp my way up the stairs to my pad. Shit. Why didn't the florist tell me that you only give lilies to dead people?

CHAPTER 20

Allison and I sit in the Mercedes, listening to Mozart and looking out over the city lights, which gleam into infinity with a million dreams and disappointments.

"Wow," I say, astonished. "It's so beautiful from up here."

"Isn't it?" The closeness of Allison's hand sends sparks up and down my arm. She turns toward me, her eyes piercing right through me. "When Kay left me, I thought I'd never be able to breathe again. But Peter is the one I miss. We used to have such fun. God, we laughed all the time. But work took over. I don't think we said more than a good morning in the last three years."

"When did you get divorced?"

"Four months ago. Things were getting too complicated. They still are, I suppose. Peter's a gentleman, but Kay won't leave me alone."

"I'm sorry."

"Don't be."

"Is there anything I can do? Like call the house and warn you she's coming up the driveway?"

She laughs. "You do quite enough, thank you."

"I don't do anything."

"You make me laugh. Barging in on that big dinner. The lilies . . . you're so innocent for your age."

"How'd you know about the lilies?"

She says nothing, only smiles.

"Believe me, I'm not very innocent."

"Oh, but you are." She turns the radio off, then leans her head against the head rest and closes her eyes.

If I could just touch her right now; I mean, I want to touch her so badly, my fingers are humming. Suppose I casually take a deep breath, then lean over and kiss her? Yeah, that'd be good. I slowly bend toward her, place a hand on her face, and kiss her, not letting go until she responds.

"Are you trying to seduce me?" she whispers.

"I think so." I kiss her again. "Why don't we move to the back seat?"

She steps out of the car; I crawl over the seat. We face each other, not talking, just staring. She pulls off her shirt, never once removing her gaze from me. She grabs my arms and pulls me on top of her. I graze my lips along her jawline and whisper, "I don't actually believe this is happening."

She moans, holds me tight, and roughly kisses my neck. "How does this feel?" she asks.

"Wonderful."

We roll over. Her hair falls across my face and chest; its softness makes me shudder. She yanks my jeans down to my hips, then wraps herself around me. I feel I am floating high above all those twinkling lights, high above the smog. We swirl together over the city until all the separate lights become one.

Her hands and lips and fingers touch every part of me, until I cry out. I have wanted this so much. We speed down toward earth, and I manage to breathe out "Wow."

She lays the back of her hand softly on my cheek. "Mmm. That was nice. It's been awhile."

"It was incredible. You're incredible. I can't believe . . . God, I love you. I totally love you. I'd do anything for you."

Silence. Dead silence.

It dawns on me that I may have made a terrible mistake, and am about to be rejected. Why didn't I keep my big mouth shut? And why does this car suddenly feel very, very small?

"Could we talk about this later?" she asks. "I'm just not sure I can handle this right now. I have some work to do, back at the house. I wasn't expecting quite an outpouring like this."

"Sure. Of course we can talk about it later. I'm sorry."

"Don't ever be sorry for what you feel." She lifts my chin and gives me a slight kiss, first on one cheek, then on the other. Then she reaches for her shirt. "Would you drive?"

We wind along the mountain road; Allison sits quietly and just looks out the window.

"Are you okay?" I ask.

"Hmm? Yes, of course." She places a hand on my leg, but its touch feels preoccupied. The shield around her stands as visible as rock and just as hard.

At home, she gets out of the car and walks toward her door. She obviously wants to be alone.

"Thank you," I say.

"I'm sorry, I just—" She walks over to me and takes my hand. "Good night."

We go our separate ways. I know I should feel ecstatic about this evening. But I don't. Not completely. Part of me feels incredible (and I mean beyond the obvious body buzz), yet the rest of me somehow feels a little cheap. I wish I knew why.

CHAPTER 21

Sometimes I hate answering machines. "You've reached Mark and Jeff. No one can come to the phone right now, so leave your name and number at the beep . . ."

"Hi, Jeff, it's Mutt. I'm just calling to say I'll be at your going-away party, and I wanted to know if I should bring anything. Oh, and I have an Allison update, though I'm sure you're not interested. Anyway, that's all. Bye."

I hang up. He probably won't call me back, being, as he is, a traitor and a jerk.

Man, I am so bored. I don't have anyone to talk to. Thank God I bought a twelve-pack of beer and a couple packs of cigarettes. Something to do. I flip on the TV, but there's just the same infomercials that were on twenty minutes ago.

I know, I'll call Diane. We have to talk. I miss her more than I would like to admit. Hopefully, Megan the Bitch hasn't tainted my image too much. I pick up the phone and call. Fourteen rings.

"Hello?"

Did I dial the right number? "Hello?" I ask.

There's a yawn, then a sleepy "Hello?"

What time is it? I check my watch. Oh, shit, 2:33 a.m. I hang up. Oops.

I guess I could go to sleep. I look at the four walls of my spacious living room. I wonder how wide it is? I pick a corner and begin a heel-toe measurement. Oh, interesting. Twenty-three "Mutt" feet. Well, let's see . . . what to do next? This restlessness is all Allison's fault. I mean, how can I sleep, not knowing how she feels about me? She expects me to sleep after the Mercedes incident?

Okay, I'll watch one of the videos I rented a few days ago. Ooh, *Terminator 2.* That'll keep my interest. Well, Linda Hamilton's muscles will keep my interest. I pull the vid out of its case and pop it in the machine.

"What in the hell are you doing?"

I jump twenty feet in the air. Literally. Who the fuck just said that? I spin around to check out the room and am appalled to find my MOTHER sitting on the couch.

"Mother, what the hell? You're DEAD!"

"No shit, Muriel."

This cannot be happening. I must be wasted. How many beers have I had? Four? No, five, but who's counting?

"I'm counting."

"What?"

"Look, Muriel, here's the deal. You have screwed up your life. What are you doing with yourself? Throwing yourself at the feet of that Beverly Hills bitch, working in a dead-end job, with no ambitions."

"This flips me out, Mother! I can't even listen to you, because you're not really here. You're a product of too much alcohol."

"You never did listen to me. Except about going to college. Thank you for giving in to me on that. But, sweetie, really, anthropology?"

I stick my fingers in my ears, close my eyes, and try to block out her voice by singing "Do-Re-Mi" at the top of my lungs.

"Oh, sweetie, that's clever—"

"—a female deer, Re, a drop of—I can't hear you!"

"Fine, Muriel. Keep singing. I'll just invade your thoughts."

"—long, long way to—no, don't do that. I'll shut up."

This is ridiculous. My dead mother is sitting on my couch, looking just the way I remember her: blowzy dyed-red hair, blue housecoat, and 50 pounds overweight. "Mother, how come you couldn't get a better dye job in heaven?"

"Don't disparage the dead. What you go up with, you stay with. Muriel, make sure you're dressed to the nines when you eat it. And I'm not here to discuss me; I'm here to talk about you."

"Lecture me is more like it."

"If that's what you want to think, fine."

"That's what I think."

"Whatever. Just listen. You're a mess, sweetie. I'm warning you, if you continue along this path of least resistance, you will have thrown away any potential you might have had. I'm going to say this one time, and one time only: don't follow in my footsteps."

"Believe me, I won't."

"You're already headed that way. Get a real job, find a nice girl, and make something of yourself."

"Find a nice girl? You spent my entire teenage years forcing Freddie Lefkowitz on me."

"He was from a good family."

"Why? Because his family's trailer was one hundred feet further away from the train tracks?"

"Freddie was a nice kid. And from what my sources tell me, he's got a successful future in the plumbing business. Keep that in mind."

"He was seven feet one and stupid. He's in jail now for armed robbery. They caught him putting gas in his car across the street from the 7-Eleven he had just robbed."

"Oh. What a shame. I guess I need new sources."

"And I am making something of myself."

"Yeah, you're making yourself a loser. Why can't you be more like your sister?"

"I'd rather die than be like her. No offense."

"Sandra's perfect."

"She's not. She has Teflon for brains. Besides, she hates me."

"She does not."

"Mom, I don't want to be a Yuphead like Sandra."

"You have nothing, Muriel. Nothing. Big-O Zero. You're embarrassing me. So much potential—"

"That's it. Get out of my house!"

"You're throwing your dead mother out?"

"I'm sick of being an embarrassment to you! Who was there when you died, huh? Was it your sweet little Sandra? No, it was me, Mother. Me."

"Honey, I appreciate all the time and effort you—"

"Get out. Get out get out get out!"

"I've gotta hit the road, anyhow. See ya, sweetie! And know I love you . . ."

Whoa. She's gone. Apartment empty. *T2* blares from the TV, and Linda Hamilton is shooting at everything in sight. Damn, I must have fallen asleep. I stumble into the kitchen for a glass of water, drink it, then splash my face with cold water.

Jesus. Housecoats in heaven? Totally pathetic.

CHAPTER 22

Mark talks to two guys with shaved heads, one of whom sports a solid-gold nose ring, while the other models a diamond lip stud. Must be friends from the Butthole, that gem of modern humanity. This going-away party has gone on for two hours, and I have only talked to Jeff for a total of thirty seconds. I'm getting tired of waiting for him to notice me and am definitely sick of the disco retreads that are spewing out of the boom box. I think a national holiday should be declared when gay men decide to abandon disco for, I don't know, Lithuanian folk music.

Squashed in a corner, surrounded by moving boxes, I grab Jeff's shirt sleeve as he walks by.

"Hey, Jeff, ever thought of paying attention to your supposed best friend?"

"Oh, my God, I've been looking all over for you. Wow, nice dress. I don't think I've ever seen you in a dress."

"You like it? I got it from Allison. She got rid of some clothes and asked if I wanted anything. You should see the killer silk suit I inherited."

"I guess I was wrong about her."

"It's okay. Hey, listen, um, I made you—"

"Honey, am I going to miss you at the gym!"

"Hi, Rick," Jeff says, uncomfortably. He manages to shrug Rick off, at which point Rick braces himself against the wall for balance. "You remember Mutt?"

"No," Rick hiccups. He looks glazedly at Jeff, then screws his face into a semblance of grief. "I'm going to miss you," he whines. Then he looks at me. "Wait a minute," he says, his face lighting up with alcohol-induced joy. "Your name's Mutt? You're Allison's new project. That's right."

"Project? I just rent her garage apartment."

"Oh, honey, Allison loves to rescue waifs. It makes for great office gossip, as they invariably fall head over heels in love—or lust—with her."

I glance at Jeff; he's got "I told you so" written all over his face. In neon pink. I'd like to crack my beer bottle over Rick's head, but refrain and mutter politely, "Well, Rick, nice seeing you. Hope to never see you again."

I hear Rick say, "Huh?" as Jeff and I move towards the bedroom.

"Can you believe him?" I exclaim. "The guy is obviously plowed. This isn't like Dickens, you know, where rich people rescue starvelings. How stupid can he get? You don't think it's true, do you? I mean, really, be honest with me— that's not what you think Allison is doing, do you? Do you?"

Jeff gives me a thoughtful stare, then says, "I think he's probably just drunk."

"Oh, man, you don't know how relieved I am to hear you say that! I knew it wasn't true."

"Here, Mutt, I have a present for you."

"You do? I have one for you, too."

I dig a tape out of my jean jacket. "I recorded all my favorite 'girl group' songs for you. For the car. See? I labeled it 'Girls for the Road.' So it'll remind you of me."

"Wow, thanks. I can't wait to hear it." Jeff reaches into the almost empty closet and pulls out a box wrapped in newspaper. "I didn't have any wrapping paper. Sorry."

I rip the paper off. In the box is the *Gertrude Stein, Gertrude Stein, Gertrude Stein* album. I slide to the floor, clutching the album to my chest.

"I can't deal with this, Jeff. What will I do without you?"

"And I want you to have my leather jacket."

When he gives it to me, I bury my face in it and sob. Sitting down beside me, Jeff wraps an arm around my shoulders to comfort me.

"It's going to be all right, Mutt. Really. I promise I'll call you every night."

"I don't want you to go! And I'm so sorry we've been fighting."

"Shhh, now, stop crying."

"I'll never forgive Mark for this. Never."

"Don't blame Mark. We both want to go."

"I know." I wipe my nose with the back of my hand and take a few ragged breaths. "I'm sorry for crying, Jeff. I didn't mean to. I really want to be supportive."

"You are, Mutt."

"I don't think I can stay any longer. This is too much for me."

"You sure?"

"Yeah."

"Okay."

We stand up and hug for a long, long time.

"You promise you'll call me?" I ask.

"Yeah, I promise."

"Will you miss me?"

"More than anything."

"Promise?"

"Promise."

"Jeff, you are the best friend anyone could ever have."

"So are you, Mutt. So are you."

❖   ❖   ❖

The road and stoplights blur dangerously through my watery tears. I can barely coordinate my body, which makes braking a bit of a nightmare. I'm wearing Jeff's jacket, and every time I focus on it, a new batch of tears starts rolling down my cheeks. I don't know where I'm going or what I'm doing; I'm just driving.

I turn down a quiet side street and stop the Blazer. I pound the steering wheel; I stomp my feet. Forcing myself to calm down, I take deep, even breaths. Okay, that helps. I look out on the houses. Well, Diane's house. I could really use some comfort right now, and she's the only one I know who can make me feel all right. I get out of the car and approach the front door. There's no answer to my knock. Too exhausted to make the trek back to my car, I sit on the front stoop.

The door opens. "Muriel? What are you doing here? It's one in the morning."

"Look, I'm sorry about the time, but Jeff's leaving tomorrow, and I'm too upset to drive any farther. Could I come in?"

Without a moment's pause, she reaches for my hand and says, "Of course you can."

Leading me into the bedroom, she sits me on the bed and helps me take off my jacket. "Would you like some tea?"

"No, that's okay."

"Do you want to talk?"

I shake my head. "Would you just hold me, please?"

"Sure."

She folds her arms around me and rocks me gently back and forth. She kisses my forehead, then puts her smooth cheek next to mine. I lay my head on her shoulder.

"Do you want to stay here tonight, Muriel?"

I nod.

"All right. Why don't you take off your clothes? I'll get you a pair of pajamas."

"Your pajamas are too small."

"Actually, these aren't—never mind. They'll fit."

She hands me a pair of green silk shorts and a tank top. She looks at me questioningly. "Is the sofa all right?"

"Um, I'd rather stay with you, if that's okay."

She smiles.

We slip under the covers, and I cling to her body.

"I can't stand people leaving me," I whisper.

"Turn over and I'll rub your back."

Her hand is so soft as it moves along my spine.

"I helped my mom die. I gave her the morphine. Do you know what it's like to watch someone die? Sandra called me a murderer. Maybe she's right. Am I talking too much? I'm a little drunk."

"You're fine."

"Mmm, that's nice. You're so good to me, Diane."

I dissolve into a restless sleep.

❖   ❖   ❖

"I'm really sorry about waking you up last night."

"Don't worry about it."

"Diane, I feel so lost."

We're sitting on her patio, with the sun beating down on us. I should be sweating, but I can't seem to shake off the chill I've had since saying good-bye to Jeff.

"You're not lost," she answers. "Well, maybe slightly."

"In what way?"

"Let's not talk about it."

"No, Diane, I want to."

"Okay." She takes a deep breath, then says, "This is just my opinion, okay? I think you don't know what you want."

"In terms of what?"

"In terms of everything. In terms of life. In terms of goals. In terms of passion."

"So, basically, in terms of everything."

"Don't get defensive. You asked what I thought, so I'm telling you."

"All right. Tell me all the ways I'm fucked up."

"You're not fucked up! God, you are so hard on yourself. You just need to figure out what you want to do. What you want out of life. And who you want in your life. I won't lie to you; I'd like to be a part of that life. But if not, I'll survive."

"Diane, I do know what I want in life."

"Okay, what?"

"Well . . . I guess I want to be someone else. I'm sick of being Mutt."

"I hate that name."

"Why? It fits."

"No, it doesn't."

"It does."

"It doesn't!"

"Okay, I don't want to argue," I say. "I don't have a clue what I'm supposed to do with this life. Are we all supposed to do fabulous and creative things? Maybe I'm one of the majority of Americans who do absolutely nothing with their mediocre lives. Maybe this is my genetic destiny. I don't know. I'm not special, Diane. I am completely ordinary. Oh, shit, I'm crying again. I hate to cry."

"Look, you've had a really hard time. Your best friend just left. You should cry."

"Hey, I know. Let's go to a movie today. That'll take my mind off things."

"Well," Diane hesitates, "I'd like to, but I already have plans. I'm meeting someone later."

"Who?"

"Megan."

"She hasn't left yet? Cancel."

"No, Muriel, I can't."

"I'm being selfish and self-centered, right?"

"I have other plans. That's all."

"Sure. I guess I better go. Sorry again for barging in last night."

She follows me into the living room, where I collect my jacket and keys. I expect her to stop me, to say she'll change her plans, but after a brief hug by the Blazer, I realize she won't.

"Hey, um, don't tell Megan you saw me, okay? I think she's got a hit man after me."

I drive away, watching Diane shrink to nothing in the rearview mirror.

CHAPTER 23

This is just ridiculous. Not a week after Jeff's departure, I'm saddled with training a new waitron. Nothing like salt on a wound. Her name is Tiffany. Tiffany. Enough said.

However, once I see her, I have to give her credit for trying to rise above (or dip below) the "Tiffany" stereotype. Instead of the requisite loafers, she stomps around in biker boots. Instead of pony-tailed blonde hair, she sports a pink buzz cut. Instead of pearl earrings, glow-in-the-dark skeletons hang heavily from her lobes. And instead of Newport Beach, she calls Reseda home.

I'm impressed at how quickly she grasps the complex concepts of the morning setup. But she's probably just being a good Do-Bee to impress the rest of us burnouts who don't really care if there's dried food on the forks.

She shadows me on a couple orders, then I set her free to take half my section. See, I don't have a problem sharing my tips, unlike some of the other waiters. Even Jeff was stingy with tips; he always groused about giving the busboys their 10%. I personally never understood that. These guys work twice as hard as us for half the money. It only seems right to share. But I'm in the minority on that opinion.

❖ ❖ ❖

I get home after a long and trying day, only to find a note from Josepha Stalin taped to my door.

"I noticed the pool was not cleaned on Friday. Please clean today."

This really ticks me off. Why doesn't this woman get off my back? I'm sick of having to kowtow to her snotty arrogance. Who the hell does she think I am? Some slave? Like it matters if I clean the pool at 8 a.m. on Friday.

I march down the stairs and, without knocking, enter the kitchen. I see Mrs. Schaber using a meat cleaver to cut celery. She would.

"Have you cleaned the pool?"

"No, I haven't," I retort, braced for battle.

"You are a day late, you know."

"Look, nobody's used the pool all week, no stupid dinner parties are coming up, Allison doesn't care, and I don't think it needs cleaning, okay?"

"You agreed, in writing, to clean that pool twice a week. I expect you to be responsible and live up to that contract."

"What are you, my mother?"

"No, thank God."

"You know what, Mrs. Schaber? I am sick of you telling me what to do. You treat me like shit, and I am not your servant."

"I never said you were."

"Oh, but you think it. 'You can't use the pool today.' 'You can't smoke in the house.' 'Use the back door.' Who do you think I am?"

Mrs. Schaber slams down the cleaver, which makes me pause for a second. She glares at me, then walks over to the phone. "How dare you yell at me? If you don't get out of this house right now, I am going to call the police."

"Go ahead, call the fucking police! What, they're going to arrest me for not cleaning the pool? Yeah, right. I will clean the pool when I want! And I expect to be treated with some respect! You act like you own this place. I'm so sick of you! That's right, pick up the phone; why don't you dial 1-800-FUCK-YOU! That's it, call the police, go ahead!"

"Allison O'Malley, please. I'll hold."

That knocks the wind right out of my sails. "You called Allison? Why'd you do that?"

She ignores me. "Yes, please have her call her housekeeper."

She sets the phone down and fixes me with a triumphant stare. She is the color of steel, from her hair to her eyes to her rigid lips.

"Don't think you've won," I say.

"When you break the agreement, you break the lease."

"Why do you have to be so mean to me? I haven't done anything to you."

"I am tired of taking care of Ms. O'Malley's rescue missions. The sooner I can get you out, the better. It's nothing personal."

"I think it's very personal. And I don't need rescuing."

I stride out the door and double lock myself in the apartment. I shouldn't have yelled at her; I know it. Now she'll get Allison to evict me from the most perfect residence in the city. What is happening to me? The jangling of the phone startles me. It's probably the commandant ordering me poolside. I yank the phone off the hook.

"I'm not cleaning the pool until you apologize!" I yell.

"Mutt?"

"Jeff? You called! Where are you?"

"Flagstaff. Mutt, it's so beautiful here. Pine trees, blue skies, and no traffic. You'd love it."

"I wish I had come with you."

"Me, too."

"Your replacement at work is a punked-out babe named Tiffany."

"They've already replaced me?"

"Sad, huh?"

"So, are you doing okay without me? Sounds like you're in the midst of a revolution."

"Oh, I've been screaming at the housekeeper, who is now going to boot me from this place. And I'm really ticked off that people keep calling me Allison's pet improvement project. And—"

"Wait, hold on a minute. What, Mark? Okay, look, I gotta go. We're meeting Mark's cousin in Prescott. I'll call you later, okay?"

"No, I really need to talk about my problems."

"It'll all work out. I'll call you tomorrow."

"But, Jeff—"

"Sorry, Mutt, gotta go. Love you."

Click.

Even though he couldn't talk for long, I feel better having heard his voice.

Now, I'd better remedy this pool situation.

❖　❖　❖

When Allison finally pulls in the driveway, I run down the stairs to intercept her before Mrs. Schaber turns me in.

"Allison, hi. Got a minute?"

"Sure. If it's just a minute. I'm running late."

"It's plenty. Look, I'll clean the pool. I just don't want Mrs. Schaber breathing down my neck every minute."

"I'm sorry?"

"I know she wants to kick me out. But she didn't have to call me your 'rescue mission.' I mean, really."

"Is that why she phoned today?"

"You haven't talked to her?"

"No, I was going to see her now."

I take a deep breath. "Was she right? About me being a rescue mission?"

"What are you talking about?"

"Oh, good. That's what I hoped you'd say."

"I'm not following."

"See, two different people have now told me that you've sort of devised a plan to rescue me."

"Who told you that?" she says sharply.

"It doesn't matter. I just want to make sure it isn't true."

"Of course not. I like to do what I can for people, that's all. I thought you might benefit from some help."

"Wait a minute, like what kind of help?"

"Well, you were living in a terrible neighborhood, and you didn't have a car, so I gave you a new start. That sort of help."

"Uh-huh." I'm getting mad now. "So, what was next? Teaching me how to talk properly? Or fuck properly?"

"Please don't bring that up."

"Don't bring what up? That we made love—no, excuse me—fucked in your car? That you let me think you cared about me?"

"I do care about you."

"You think you can play with people, don't you? I know I'm not the only loser you've tried to save. Was Kay one of your pets? Do you sleep with everyone you rescue?"

"Mutt, please—"

"I loved you, Allison. How stupid can I be?"

"You're not stupid. Don't say that."

"Do you deny leading me on? Do you?"

"I was vulnerable."

"You were not vulnerable. You were using me, because that's what you do with people. It's like when people order side dishes at the restaurant. They want it, they take one small bite, they forget about it, then I have to throw it away. You could feed half of Ethiopia with the side dishes I throw in the garbage."

"What are you talking about?"

"I'm talking about—I don't know what I'm talking about."

I look at her through a completely clear lens. She stands, hand on her hip, in her tailored suit. Still the perfect hair, glinting in the orange glow of sunset. Her eyes still a soft hazel, her lips still full and seemingly kind. Seemingly. Seemingly flawless, faultless, and sublime. I've let myself be had.

"You wanted someone to make you feel better about yourself," I say.

"Mutt, let's talk about this. It's really not what you're thinking. I do find you attractive."

"Bullshit."

"Mutt—"

"My name is Muriel. Get it? Muriel."

"I'm sorry, Muriel."

"I don't want to talk to you ever again. I'm giving my notice. Go find another sucker to play Pygmalion with."

Have you ever heard the saying that an obsession is like a penny? If you hold a penny right up to your eye, it's the only thing you can see. But it ain't worth much.

CHAPTER 24

What did I just do? I'm now completely homeless. And worse, carless. I'm going to have to get a cab to move my stuff. And move it to where? Maybe my old apartment's still available and not occupied by squatters. I'll check on it first thing tomorrow morning. And Jeff's not even here to help.

I can't believe I just hoisted myself out of the best deal in Beverly Hills. So I had to clean the pool. Yeah, I also had to deal with a perpetually PMSing housekeeper. So what? I had a car; I had skylights; I had a VCR, for God's sake.

I gotta get away from this mess of my own creation. If I hurry, I can catch the bus to the Rifle. I'll hang out, watch people dance, and have a few beers to take my mind off my misery.

Man, integrity sucks.

❖   ❖   ❖

Sitting at the dark end of the bar, I gaze at a myriad laughing faces. Who are these people? Are they single and looking? Coupled and lonely? Rich? Poor? Angry? Ecstatic?

Who knows. Each face seems to be a painted mask of false and desperate gaiety.

The bartender slaps down drinks and scoops up money as fast as humanly possible. He works his way from one end of the long bar to the other; by the time he gets back to the beginning, everyone has an empty glass and he has to start pouring and scooping all over again. He smiles, sometimes winks, and every so often blows out a breath of boredom. Or weariness. He reminds me of Sisyphus, pushing that rock up the hill just to watch it roll back down again.

The music cranks up a few decibels, now that it's prime time. The bass beat shakes the floor and screws with the natural rhythm of my heart. I wonder if the rapidly changing beats have ever caused arrhythmia or a heart attack. I don't doubt it.

I gulp my beer, then check the bar bunch again. It's a sea of new faces, dotted by a few old-timers deep in conversations or far too drunk to move. A couple of women wait for drinks at the far end of the bar. They don't stay, though. There has always been a mutual hostility when a member of the opposing gender invades one or the other of the rooms. They say gay men and women have been united, spurred by their activism around AIDS, but, if truth be told, segregation is the acceptable and comfortable norm. At least in this joint.

I wrap Jeff's jacket tightly around me. Not to stay warm: it's about 113 degrees in here. The jacket gives me a sense of protection and peace. I can pretend Jeff is twenty paces away, dancing his heart out with the other boys. I wish I could have gone with him. If it wasn't for Mark-the-Butthole, I'd probably be cruising across the Midwest with my best buddy. Hey, maybe I should hop a Greyhound and join them. Chicago can't stink any worse than this pit.

Unfortunately, my life probably wouldn't be much different, though: waitressing, tiny apartment, bar, crime, smog, traffic. Forget it. Why move across the country to encounter the same miserable environment? And the truth is, Jeff never asked me to go.

"Hey, looking to score some coke?"

I swivel my head to look at a lanky, pockmarked, toothless dinghead, whose ammonia breath makes me want to gag.

"Are you talking to me?" I ask, disgusted.

"$100."

"What?"

He leans perilously close to my nose and says, "Good stuff."

"I don't do drugs. You're probably a cop, anyway. I happen to be an aficionado of that TV show."

"Forget it, then."

"Don't worry, I will."

I watch him walk down the line of people at the bar. The fifth guy he approaches nods briefly, then follows the dealer out the door. By the time I lose interest, about ten people have taken him up on his offer. You can't go anywhere these days without running into some illegal activity. What a world.

This music's giving me a headache. I wonder if Diane's home. Maybe I'll give her a call. No, can't do that. She'd think I was using her. Yet, I really do want to see her. She's so nice to me. Not like that bitch, Allison, who pictured me as some bedraggled cat in need of a bath and a bowl of food.

I slide off my barstool and maneuver my way through the crowds. As I turn the corner onto Santa Monica Boulevard, I have to detour around a true crime scene. Kneeling on the pavement, facing the brick wall, hands over their heads, are the suckers who followed Mr. Plainclothes out for a snort. I knew it. I am, however, disappointed at the lack of TV cameras. I would have loved for Sister Sandra to see my face on national television. I spot our fearless undercover agent in the crowd. He looks up from writing his report and mutters, "Say no to drugs."

"Trust me, I do." God, after that experience at Denise's barbecue, I'd never touch them again.

I have to say, I've always felt safe walking along the Boulevard. That says a lot for West Hollywood. Aside from gay bashing, petty carjacking, and burglary, you could mistake this place for a small town. I breathe in the smoky air, lengthen my stride, and relax into the light foot traffic.

"Hey, girlfriend!"

"Tiffany!"

My new coworker pulls up next to me in a beat-up red Bug, top down, music blaring. It makes me so happy to see a familiar face that I practically fall down and kiss the dirty sidewalk.

"Watcha doing?" she asks.

"Nothing much."

"I'm heading for Chicktown; wanna go?"

"Really? Isn't that way out in West L.A.?"

"Yeah, it's cool. Hop in."

I hesitate for about a fourth of a second, then jump in the car. Tiffany revs the little engine, causing the car to backfire, then squeals away from the curb, without signaling or looking behind her for oncoming traffic.

"Hey, Tiffany, you did pretty good at work today."

"Like I give a shit about that piece-of-shit job. Hang on, I'm gonna run the light."

I can't answer her cynicism, as we are about to be run over by a sofa delivery truck.

"Hey, watch out!"

"Yes!" she yells, obviously exhilarated by her brush with death. I just wish she wasn't taking me on the tour with her.

"Um, Tiffany, could you slow down?"

"Okay, Grandma."

"Ha ha."

"Mellow out."

"I just want to live to see the sun rise."

"This is a great tune. Check it out!"

And, of course, she turns the radio up to the noise level of a Dead concert. I think I'm getting heart murmurs.

Besides having a frightening name, Chicktown is housed in a frightening warehouse in the middle of what I consider to be nowhere. But, then again, all of West L.A. is a vast nowhere to me. As we approach the building, silence surrounds us.

"Um, you sure it's open?" I ask.

"It's cool. Come on."

Inside, the place is a trip. Black walls, black floor, black bar, dyed-black hair, black polyester. Oh, and just to vary the chromatic scheme, an ebony dance floor.

"Tiff—do you mind if I call you that?" She shakes her head and I continue, "How about if I buy you a drink?"

"Cool. I'll have a Black Russian."

I have to stop myself from rolling my eyes.

We get our drinks (I stick with my standard draft, which costs more here than anywhere else in the western world), and walk over to the edge of the dance area. Well, what I figure is the edge. Disney villainesses slink around the floor. Along the back wall, I see three cylindrical cages, which, I kid you not, house go-go dancers wrapped in chains. I'm sorry, I'm shocked.

I turn to Tiff and say, "Do you get the symbolism of that image? What's the deal? Whatever happened to feminism?"

"Feminism?" she sneers. "The movement that gave rise to an increase in the nun population? That viewed sex as a sin worse than Catholicism? Give me a break!"

"Look, um, I've never been a feminist or anything, but this cage thing really bothers me."

"Get over it. It's the empowerment of women through disempowerment."

"What?"

"Wanna have sex?"

"What?!"

"Just asking. You're cute, I'm horny, why not?"

"What?!"

"I guess that's a no-go."

"I need another beer."

I've got to get out of this catacomb now. And I don't mean now as in right now; I mean now as in yesterday. This place is a sepulcher of the strange and undead. And they play disco. I can't escape it. Instead of getting a beer, I walk back over to Tiffany.

"Look, Tiffany, I'm really tired. And this music is not my style. Could you please take me home?"

"Oh, come on, stay and party."

"Don't you have to work tomorrow?"

"Yeah, don't you?"

"No. I just want to go home. Please."

Her teeth look ghoulish in the black light.

"Okay," she says. "For a price."

"You want me to put gas in your car? No problem."

"Come home with me."

"Are you kidding?"

"That's the price. Take it or leave it."

"Well, I guess I'll call a cab."

She sidles up next to me and runs her hand along the inside of my thigh.

"What are you doing?"

"Trying to tempt you."

"Look, we don't know each other at all."

"Okay, we can take it slow. Wanna dance? Next hour, it's Open Cage Dancing."

"Tiff, you know what? It's been great fun, but I gotta go. Sorry. Um, where's the phone?"

She points to the hallway leading to the restrooms, and I take off like a racewalker. Oh, perfect, the phone's red. What a decorating idea. I call a cab, then sneak out the front door.

God, what I would give for normalcy right now. My life is a shambles, and the whole world seems off-kilter. I shake the weirdness out of my head, light a cig, and wait for a cab to whisk me away from this ordeal.

CHAPTER 25

Mom, I'm falling apart. This cab smells of stale cigars, and the acrid stink reminds me of my own stale life. Outside the car window, I watch the Bev Hills fortresses go by, gated and massive. Each house has a cheap facade, and the pretension doesn't impress me anymore.

You can't count on anyone, Mom. They either control you or leave you. I feel I've aged fifty years in the past couple weeks. I feel too tired to go on.

So, where's the path, Mom? I'm afraid. Afraid of others and of myself. I want to count on something, anything. I need to feel okay.

Why aren't you here to love me?

CHAPTER 26

I pay the driver, run up the steps, and start pounding. Please open the door, please open the door, please open the door. I pound again.

"Are you going to make a habit of this?" Diane asks after opening the door.

"I have to talk to you!"

"Then come in off the porch."

We walk inside and Diane sits on the couch.

"Diane, I am so happy to see you." I walk from one side of the room to the other, thoroughly agitated.

"Please stop pacing," she says through a yawn. "And take off your jacket. What's going on?"

"Okay, okay, listen, this is really important. In the cab tonight, I was almost at my house, but I had to see you. So here I am."

"And?"

"I want to go to the Arboretum with you."

"You came over in the middle of the night to tell me that?"

"No, no. I want to read your poetry. All of it. I want to watch *The Blinding Light* with you. I want to have coffee with you. I want to look at your face with that big, goofy, sweet smile. I want to see the pictures you took of those flowers. I never asked to see them. I've been horrible to you. I've been selfish and mean and rotten and cruel. I don't know, I just—you've never let me down, Diane. You're decent. And that's rare. I can't lose that."

Worn out from my speech, I collapse into a chair and wait.

"Bravo, what a performance!"

I turn towards the voice coming from the doorway.

"Megan?" I jump up and turn towards Diane. "What's she doing here?"

"What does it look like I'm doing here?" Megan asks. Her hair is wet and she's wearing those green silk pajamas. I look at Diane. Her hair is wet and she's wearing a robe.

"What the hell is going on?" I ask them both.

"Well—" Diane starts.

"You might as well be a good little girl and head on home," Megan says.

"Don't tell me what to do. And get out of our conversation. This is private."

"Diane and I don't have secrets. So I'll just sit on the couch and you'll never know I'm here."

She sits. No one says anything.

It's so quiet, the dissonant ticking of all the clocks in the house sounds as loud as being underneath a 747 at takeoff.

Finally, Diane opens her mouth and slowly says, "You decided all this stuff in the space of a cab ride?"

"Well, it was from West L.A. I really thought this through and—"

"Ha!"

I whirl toward Megan. "Be quiet! You're supposed to pretend you're not here."

"Megan, could you please leave us alone for a minute?" Diane asks.

Megan glares at me, shakes her head, then huffs off to the bedroom.

"Could you shut the door, please?" I yell after her.

Megan slams the door. Hard.

"What the hell is going on, Diane? I thought you wanted me."

Diane stares at the floor.

"Well, don't you?"

"Muriel, you strung me along, even though you're in love with someone else. That's lying."

"You mean Allison? She's out of my life. I've given notice, and in the morning, I'm going to find a new place to live."

"What do you mean, you gave notice?"

"Since when have you and Megan—I mean, I know she's your friend, but she's totally arrogant."

"I heard that!" Megan says through the door.

"Oh, go take another shower!"

"Muriel—"

"Look, Diane, Allison is history. She means nothing to me. I swear to you. Please, can't we start over?"

"Muriel—"

"Please, Diane. You don't want to be with Megan. Come on, you'll never see her. You said yourself she only breezes through town. But me? I'll be here every day."

"Mur—"

"Diane, you've got to trust me. I need you. I need to be with you."

"Stop interrupting me! You waltz in here and expect me to be overjoyed by the fact that you need me. You only want me because you can't have Allison. Because you don't have Jeff. You don't want me for me; you want me to replace someone else. You want me to take care of you and say I love you. Until something better comes along."

"I told you she had that mother issue!" Megan screams.

I walk to the bedroom door. "Shut up!"

"I deserve to be loved for who I am," Diane continues. "I won't be anyone's replacement. I'm sorry. So, thank you for the impassioned speech, but it's not enough."

"Well, what is enough? How can I show you I want to be with you? Tell me."

Diane sighs, glances toward the bedroom, then rests her gaze on me. "I don't know, Muriel."

Looking at her lovely, troubled face, I realize there may be an inkling of truth in all she said. But just an inkling.

CHAPTER 27

Tiffany's advances begin to border on sexual harassment. Every day this week, she has either thrown a lewd innuendo my way or blatantly grabbed my ass. Much as I hate to admit it, I'm actually afraid of going to work. I mean, she bruised my butt when she pinched it yesterday, and I don't want the area re-injured.

I'm on the second leg of my bus ride back to Beverly Hills (having returned the keys to the Blazer), watching humanity flow past the window. It's a funny place, this city. If you walk anywhere, you're suspected of being homeless or crazy. If you take a bus, you're an out-and-out loser. Ownership of a '79 Impala affords one more status than ownership of a $1,500 bicycle. It's wacky. No other metropolis in this country has a caste system this obvious. Signs should be posted at the city limits that read: ENTERING LOS ANGELES: YOU DRIVE, THEREFORE YOU ARE.

I understand that the spread of the metropolitan area has made a car a necessary means of transport. Yet, I think it goes deeper than mere necessity. I believe people own cars in Los Angeles because they are afraid, deeply afraid. That 3,000-pound piece of tin is a defense against vulnerability.

Wrapped in steel, you can ignore the crime, whisk past the graffiti, watch a red light rather than meet the gaze of a homeless man with an outstretched hand. A car protects its cargo from the nasty, dirty, frightening underbelly of life.

I know. Being a bus traveler, I have had to keep my guard up, lest the pervasive psychic pollution attack my nervous system. Facing a stranger in L.A., trying to understand his or her world, is just too much to handle. You wonder why people peg our city as the superficial capital of the world? Trust me, it's all because of fear. We hide behind whatever we can. I'm as guilty as everyone else.

❖   ❖   ❖

I slap an address label on my third and last box so I can mail my belongings to my new digs. Well, my new old digs. When I went by the apartment building to see if I could re-rent my studio, I wasn't surprised when the manager told me it was still available. He was so desperate, he knocked fifty bucks off the rent when I promised to fix it up. He even gave me forty dollars cash, saying I could pick out the paint. What a deal. I'll do a complete make-over of the place.

I'm moving at the end of the week, and the only people interested in my new address are my boss and Stepford Sister Sandra. Kind of sad.

A car door slams. Allison must be home. Normally, I would run to the window so I could get a dose of her uncommon beauty. Not today. Today, I throw myself on the sofa, stare at the ceiling, and obsess about the fact that I was stupidly obsessed about Allison. I guess I fooled myself into thinking it was love. I guess I'm still a fool.

If only I'd seen the red flags. I should have recognized the too-much-of-a-good-thing syndrome. I should be furious with her, but I can't muster any feeling other than a dull pain. I still wish she could love me.

I have got to get out of this place. Maybe I should have gone to Tiffany's welcome party at work (a gala that she instigated herself). I got out of it earlier by saying that I was going to a screening at the Directors Guild. Of course, in reality, I picked up a six-pack and a video, planning to spend my last night here in white-trash splendor. Hey, I'm not proud.

I have the phone within reach, in case Jeff calls. Or Diane. Jeff hasn't called me since that first day he was on the road. I assume he's been too busy decorating a new apartment and finding a job to even think about getting in touch with his best friend.

I sit up at the sound of someone coming up my stairs. The door swings open, and in steps Tiffany of the wandering hands. I've been caught.

"I knew you weren't going to a screening," she announces.

I stand, keeping the couch a barrier between us.

"Actually, Tiff, I'm heading out right now. Sorry to disappoint you."

"I called the Guild. There's nothing on tonight. So I came to get you for the party."

"How'd you know where I lived?"

"I have sources."

"What are you? Agent 99?"

"I checked your employment file."

"That's illegal."

"Big fucking deal."

"You could get fired for that."

"Like I said, big fu—"

"Look, Tiff, to be honest with you, I'm feeling a bit under the weather, so I'll have to pass on the party."

"Then I'll hang with you here for a while, babe."

She approaches; I dart around to the other end of the couch.

"What's with you?" she asks. "You're acting like I'm gonna kill you or something."

"I'd prefer not to get goosed again, okay?"

"Whatever. You don't look sick. Let's go to my party."

"I don't want to go. Don't you get it?"

"Don't be such a loser. What else do you have to do?" She notices the boxes and asks, "What's up? Moving out?"

"Yep."

"You're kidding! This place is totally intense. I'd give my right tit to live here."

I pause as a humongous light bulb flashes above my head. I walk over to Tiffany and give her a big, broad, welcoming smile. Putting my arm around her shoulder, I say chummily, "Want to see the other rooms? You know, if you're interested, I could put in a good word with the housekeeper."

"You have a housekeeper?" she asks, astounded at my good fortune.

"Sure. She's really nice. You'd love her. And you're not going to believe how cheap the place is. Oh, and you even get a break on the rent if you clean the pool."

"I've never cleaned a pool before."

"It's easy," I say expansively. "Trust me."

She's taking the bait: I can see the greed in her eyes. As I show off the designer details in each room, I feel the strength of her yearning grow.

"You've got to meet the owner," I say. "She's great. And totally cute. In a movie star sort of way."

"Really?"

"Trust me."

"I want it." Tiffany's breathing heavily now.

Ah, sweet revenge. A buzz cut and a nose ring are just what this place needs.

"Let me show you the grounds," I continue smoothly.

I should be a used-car salesman. I could make a mint.

CHAPTER 28

J une 1

Dear Mom,

Well, another year has rolled around. Happy birthday. You would have been forty-eight this year, can you believe it? I put a candle in a chocolate cupcake (the kind you like, with the chocolate sprinkles) and made a wish for your happiness, wherever you are.

Anyway, just thought I'd update you on my life. As you know, I got lost on a slight detour through fantasyland, but am back on track, living in my old apartment. It's not half bad.

I'm very proud of the work I put into it. I painted the walls pale peach and highlighted the doorframes in glossy white. Sandra would be proud of me. I had some light gray carpet put down—don't worry, my landlord paid for it. Hey, my window actually opens now, so I'll be able to get fresh air. I found a bookcase and a futon at a garage sale; the place actually has a bit of class.

Mom, I hope you can see that I'm trying to make my life a little better. You've got to be patient with me, because change comes slow. And is very expensive.

I love you, and wish I could celebrate with you. As usual, I'll be sending this letter to our old address, even though they replaced the trailer park with a strip mall. I know you'll get it, somehow.

Happy Forty-eighth!

Love Always,
Muriel

CHAPTER 29

Just as I am about to give up on Jeff, I get a letter. And a Chicago Bears cap, which isn't quite my style, but, hey, don't look a gift horse in the mouth, right?

Anyway, Jeff and Mark have found a fifth-floor walk-up that is a block and a half from Jeff's new job. He's started as a busboy in a trendy vegetarian eatery, but says he's moving up to day waiter in six months. I guess it's hard to break into the restaurant business anywhere.

I fold the letter and stuff it in the breast pocket of my leather jacket. I start to put on the Bears cap, but can't quite do it. After all, here at Beans 'n the Hood, the new neighborhood coffee house, it's punk poetry night, and I don't think the cap would go over so well. Since Jeff's departure (and the loss of Diane and Allison), my social life has plummeted to the level where grocery shopping at 10:30 p.m. makes a good night out.

I am totally alone; I have no one that I can show off my redecorated apartment to. Oh, well, time to get off the pity-pot and do something besides smoke, drink espresso, and listen to poems of violence-tinted angst. I'm going to the grocery store.

I step from the smoke-filled room into the smoke-filled air. Sweating my way down the street, I cringe as the booming pseudo-music that spills from the open windows of passing cars assaults my ears. What happened to this world? I must have missed the moment when Captain and Tenille were replaced by gangsta rap. I'm telling you, life was better when it was shared with Bob and Emily.

At the entrance to the supermarket, I squeeze my way past a guy who's forcing people to sign a "Legalize Marijuana" petition. Then I'm accosted by two inebriated teenagers looking for someone to buy them beer. I ignore them and run into a mother and son trying to find homes for a boxful of kittens. I glance in the box, then stop dead in my tracks. It's Destiny. Or Destiny's Evil Russian Twin, right down to the lightning bolt of white across its raven face. I'm about to make the sign of the cross when the tiny furball mews at me. Plaintively.

"I think this one's found a family," the mother says.

"Oh, no, not me," I answer. "Cats and I do not mix."

I turn and head through the automatic doors. I get a cart and roll toward the Pop Tart aisle. Then, when I step back to take in the selection, a blood-curdling scream almost assassinates me. I look down. Oh, my God, I stepped on the kitten; it must have followed me into the store.

"Go away."

It gazes at me with mournful emerald eyes.

"Go on, get out of here."

Rolling over on its back, it stretches to twice its inky, natural length.

"Look, find another home, okay?"

It gets up, rubs against my jeans, and purrs.

Now what? The poor thing has apparently bonded. And with the completely wrong person. If I walk away, it will feel totally betrayed and then suffer from abandonment issues the rest of its life. I cannot be a party to that kind of psychological abuse.

I sigh. "Would you like to see how I redecorated my apartment?"

I pick up Destinevsky, set her (I think it's a her) in the child seat, and finish shopping.

❖   ❖   ❖

Okay, let's try this again: litter box in the bathroom, food and water bowls by the pantry, cat toys in the main room, kitten lying across my shoulders while I watch TV. I can't move in any direction without upsetting the balance, so I cleverly place my soda and cigarettes between my legs.

I slowly sneak a cigarette out of the pack. Good. Kitty's still purring. I light up; Destinevsky sneezes twice, then dives under the futon. Oh, man, I can't believe it. She's allergic to smoke. Now I'll have to go sit on the stair landing. Exiled from my own kingdom. I suppose the cat can just deal and I could stay on the couch and enjoy my cig. Yet, I crumble immediately under the statistical threat of secondhand smoke breaking apart nuclear families, so it's out to the landing I go.

❖   ❖   ❖

We've gotten into a comfortable pattern this past week. For one, she's a great alarm clock. When 6:30 rolls around, she begs for food and attention. When I leave for work, she does a figure eight around my legs, pleading for me to stay home. When I return, stressed out and tired, she greets me at the door. At night, she nuzzles against my neck and her soft breathing puts me to sleep. This cat is way better than a girlfriend. Des and I are a match made in heaven.

CHAPTER 30

I was furious. "What do you mean, I have to work on Sunday? It's the Pride Parade!"

The manager doesn't look up from his apparently important work. "Sorry, Mutt, you didn't get your request in early enough."

"What request? You know no one's going to come in. We're right next to the parade route. Nobody could get through. Besides, I have seniority. The newest waitron should work that day."

"Tiffany asked for the day off when she interviewed."

"But that's not fair!"

"I'm sorry, the schedule's set."

I slam my fists on the desk and get right in his face. "I can't believe it! I really can't believe you'd let her request take priority."

"How was I supposed to know you wanted the day off?"

"Well, duh!"

"Mutt, calm down. Why don't you see if she'll trade with you?"

"Yeah, right. Why don't we just close for the day?"

"Mutt—"

"Can I at least bring a book? Oh, forget it."

I leave the manager to his paper pushing and descend into the depths of hell that this restaurant has become with the advent of Tiffany. I glare at her as I strap on my apron. She blows me a kiss. I could slug her. Instead, I sidle up to her. Real close. I have no compunction about making a deal with the Devil's wife.

"So, Tiff. Babe. What's up?"

"Nothing much."

"How's it going at Allison's? Enjoying the peace and quiet?"

"Thanks a fucking lot."

"You like it, huh?"

"That deal with the pool? Sucks. I tried it twice, then told that blowhard housekeeper she could hire a slave for the job."

"You did?"

"Yeah. But I still have to do it. What's the deal with that Nazi?"

"I'm so sorry. I thought she was rather pleasant, myself."

"Really. At least there's Allison. Major babe."

My heart trips a little. "How is she?"

"She works too hard, she drinks too much, and she doesn't appreciate her situation."

"Ah. Look, Tiff, I need Sunday off. Could we switch?"

"You've got to be kidding!"

"I'm desperate. My mother's coming in from Seattle and . . . she's walking in the PFLAG group. It was spur of the moment. I haven't seen her in, um, a couple of years. We need to do that healing thing, you know?"

"I'll take a picture for you. No way am I gonna miss Dykes on Bikes."

"Come on, Tiff, be a pal. You understand the intricacies of familial relations, don't you?"

She looks at me with a blank expression.

"Tiff. Tiff. Let me cut you another deal. I'll work two other days for you and give you all my tips, okay?"

"No way."

I turn away from her and start setting up the salt shakers. "Fine. No problem. Guess you didn't want to go to dinner with me, huh?"

She stops on her way to the main room. "What?"

"Whatever," I say, as airily as possible.

"You're asking me out to dinner?"

"That is what I said."

"Really? Ms. Cold-as-Ice?"

"Mmm-mmm."

"Let me think about it."

I have sunk too low this time. Going out with Tiffany could end in date rape. With leather. But I'm not about to miss a Pride Parade. No way.

Then I have a typical day of fucked-up orders and lousy tips. And all of it punctuated by Tiffany suggesting the various places we could go after our "date" to make out. At five minutes to shift change, I approach her again, confident that Sunday will be mine.

"Well, have you decided?"

"Yeah, I have."

"And?"

"No go. Sorry. You'll just ask for a ride home after dessert."

"What? How do you know?"

"I know manipulation when I see it."

I'm filled with remorse for being caught in a scam, guilt for practically selling my body, and the utmost relief that I won't be caught in Tiffany's clutches.

So, I'll miss the parade. I can still go to the festival.

CHAPTER 31

I re-route on my bike this morning to avoid the crowds along Santa Monica Blvd. I don't need blatant reminders of the gala I'll be missing. Juan and I are the only staff on duty. Great. The famous silent busboy. So much for carrying on a conversation with a warm, human body.

Just thinking about all my coworkers enjoying the parade makes me seethe with jealousy. Why do I always get stuck with the shitty schedules? I had to work Christmas, for God's sake. And you can imagine what a joy it was: beef burritos do not adequately substitute for turkey and family. Well, turkey, Jeff, and, yes, even Mark.

Lounging at the bar, I open a new novel. I have to read the first page three times, as my concentration keeps getting diverted by the intermittent sounds of applause and music wafting in from the parade route. A few people meander in for coffee. Ooh, twenty-five-cent tips. Lucky me.

I have time for a leisurely brunch of black bean soup, a dinner salad, and flan—the only items we slaves are allowed to have for free. Even this no-cost meal cannot assuage my anger. Why am I here?

I take a cig out back, where I will not be disturbed. I gaze longingly through the alley toward the backs of the parade watchers. They are all getting a hint of a sunburn that will be beet red by the end of the day.

I flip the butt into the empty parking lot and shuffle back inside. Juan taps my shoulder and points to Table 8, where a man and woman are sitting side by side, holding hands and gurgling into each other's ears. I hate when couples sit like that.

"Hi," I say. "You managed to get through the crowds, I see."

The guy tilts his head back and laughs heartily. Did I say something funny?

"We live up the street," he answers, "so we strolled on down."

"Can you believe all the people out today?" I ask.

"Frankly," the woman sighs, "I don't understand the point. I mean, Joe and I don't flaunt our sexuality. Why do they get a day to flaunt theirs?"

Joe adds, "And I am so sick of those rainbow bumper stickers. Every car on our block has one."

"Hey, this is West Hollywood," I say.

"Joe and I get so irritated with this 'Pride' nonsense, don't we, honey? Where's our day to show off our heterosexuality?"

I muster a sickly smile. These two obviously don't get that every day is "Celebrate the Straight" day.

"Not that we have anything against gay people, you understand. It's just . . . well, you know."

She looks to me with this last statement, thinking I am firmly in her camp. Anybody who says they "don't have anything against" any group, clearly does. I subvert further bimbonic discussion by taking their order.

I manage to serve and usher them out in under thirty minutes. Good riddance. I hope they get heartburn from the extra Tabasco I splashed on their huevos rancheros. Yeah, yeah, I know it was immature.

"Hey, babe, how about a pitcher of margs for me and my compadres?"

Tiffany. And her clone friends. I should just poison myself right now. She's only here to rub her fabulous day in my face. All five girls wear white tanks emblazoned with the word "DYKE." Well, no shit. Like you could mistake these cretins for Orange County housewives.

"Nice shave, Tiff. Hope you didn't nick your scalp."

"Man, isn't it a riot? Totally spur of the moment. Middle of the night, we all decided to shave off our hair as an awesome statement against the fascist codes of femininity."

"I sure hope you put on sunscreen."

"Of course. We even brought baseball caps. UV light kills."

"I thought lesbian separatism died out in about, oh, 1976," I say sarcastically.

"We were thinking of streaking the parade as a protest against the gay male fashion majority."

"Why don't you just keep it simple and burn your bras?"

"No way! These Wonderbras are too expensive."

I leave the group to their drinks and sit at the other end of the bar. Tiffany follows me down, gulps her margarita, and slams the glass on the counter. I open my book as a direct signal that I don't want her company.

"Hey, babe, so like, where's your mom?"

"My mother? My mother's dead."

Tiffany goes stone-cold silent.

Finally, "You lied to me."

"About what?" I innocently ask.

"I thought your mother was marching with the PFLAG group."

"Oh, that was just a ploy to get you to change days with me. But I'm sure she's marching in spirit." I go back to my book. I am not in the frame of mind for "Let's Tell the Truth."

"What bullshit! I actually felt sorry for you."

"Whatever."

"I can't believe you!"

"Hey," I say nonchalantly, "you didn't switch, so what's the problem?"

"You're such a loser."

"Look, why don't you get off my back? I'm not in the mood for you."

"Fine." She spins on her rubber sole and waves for her friends to follow.

As the group goes through the door, I call out, "Have fun on the chain gang!"

Tiffany's eyes narrow, her jaw sets, and she takes a step towards me, like she's going to punch me out. The gaggle of girls stares at me, too. I'm afraid I'm going to become a segment of *Rescue 911* in about eight seconds.

Tiffany walks stiffly up to me, with her lips parted in a Cheshire Cat grin. "I forgot to mention, I've been seeing a lot of Allison."

I close my book and set it as casually as I can on the counter. Never let the enemy see that they've found the chink in the armor.

"I—I beg your pardon?"

"You heard me," she smirks.

"Do you think I care what you do?"

Tiffany puts her mouth next to my ear and whispers, "She's really hot in bed."

I shake my head in total disbelief. Allison and Stubblehead?

"Just thought you'd like to know. Mutt."

She walks out the door, but her maniacal laugh hangs in the ceiling corners. What a tarantula. I grip the counter edge to keep from screaming. Un-fucking-believable. The Queen of My Dreams and the Demon of My Nightmares? No way in hell. It's not true. It can't be.

I swivel around at the sound of the door opening, fully expecting Tiffany to come humiliate me with some other gem of a lie. I'm ready to maim and kill. I mean, that was my Allison. Mine. It's not fair.

"What?" I snarl.

"Hi."

The figure at the door slowly comes into focus. A girl with curly blonde hair, a Yankees cap, and a smile as big as Kansas.

"Diane," I quietly say.

"Hi." She leans awkwardly against the host stand, her hands in her pockets. Juan runs by to set chips and water on a table, then motions for her to sit.

"Hi, Diane," I say.

We stare at each other. Finally, she breaks the connection and looks at the floor. I'd say something, but I can't get my mouth to work. When she raises her gaze, her face is quite serious.

"I was in the neighborhood," she says, "and wondered if you'd like to go to the festival with me tonight."

"Aren't you meeting Megan?"

"Actually, she left for Peru a couple days ago."

"Really?"

"Do you have other plans?"

"No! I'm not off work for another two hours, though."

"I'll wait."

She'll wait. For me. Wow.

EPILOGUE

It's been two weeks since Diane walked into Mexicali Joe's and swept me off my feet. That night, we strolled through the festival, commenting only on the contents of each booth, careful not to hold each other's hand. After all, I didn't know if she just wanted company for the evening or if it was a sign that things were going to be okay between us.

Along about midnight, walking back towards the restaurant, she took my hands and pulled me into a dark doorway. Bathed in the soft breeze of a balmy summer night, we stood so close I could feel her breath on my face.

"Thank you for a wonderful evening," she whispered.

"Yeah, it was great."

Hesitantly, I leaned forward to kiss her. She slowly closed her eyes, and our lips met in the lightest, gentlest kiss imaginable. In that moment, I felt completely without fear and completely connected to another person.

In a voice so low it felt more like a vibration than a tone, I heard, "I think I love you."

And the words came from me. Wouldn't you know I'd actually quote the Partridge Family.

We spent the night at my place, wrapped in the bliss of discovering each other's newness. We were cautious, slow, and, finally, generous with our bodies. When sleep was pulling us, Desi dug under the covers and snuggled between us, her head resting on our enclasped hands. My last thought before darkness was what a comfortable little family we made.

Not everything has been perfection, though. Every day at work, I have had at least one incident where the cooks failed to make an order I had submitted. This, of course, caused customers to stiff me for poor service. Then it finally dawned on me: Tiffany had decided I was Public Enemy Number 1. She was pulling my orders and throwing them away. Clever little twit.

I went on the offensive last Thursday, retaliating by pouring sugar on her orders. It was pretty funny to watch patrons gag at the taste of their burritos. I can safely boast that I secretly sweeten at least half her food items, while she can only steal one or two of my order sheets without my noticing.

Allison came into the restaurant yesterday and gave Tiffany an aloof and perfunctory nod. This action confirmed my suspicions that Tiff had lied on that fateful parade day. Naturally, I didn't put sugar on Allison's food. I wouldn't stoop that low.

She ignored me completely.

All in all, things aren't half bad. My apartment looks great, Desi is a dream, and Diane picks me up from work every day. Not that I'm using her for a ride or anything. She wants to do it, so we don't waste any time apart. Okay, so it's a little codependent. Whatever.

We've spent every night together, splitting the time between houses. In the evening, Diane writes or grades papers while I read her poetry. It's really incredible. Although she won't let me read the series she wrote about me. That's going to drive me nuts.

So I probably look like a simpering idiot in love, and I know that somewhere, someone is making fun of me. I don't care. I like being like this. It may not last past this weekend, but the thrill is totally worth it.

I mean, who knows what lasts in this world? I thought my Saab and I would never be parted. It never crossed my mind that Jeff would abandon me. And who can tell how long I'll be able to put up with Tiffany and the restaurant?

Whatever happens, happens. Hey, life's like that, you know?

The End

About the Author

Kim Taylor lives in Boulder, Colorado. She is currently at work on her second novel, *Cissy Funk*.

If you enjoyed *Side Dish*, why not write the author and tell her so. She will be delighted to hear from you. You may send your correspondence to:

Kim Taylor
c/o Rising Tide Press
3831 N. Oracle Rd.
Tucson, AZ 85705

More Fiction to Stir the Imagination from Rising Tide Press

RETURN TO ISIS
Jean Stewart
It is the year 2093, and Whit, a bold woman warrior from an Amazon nation, rescues Amelia from a dismal world where females are either breeders or drones. During their arduous journey back to the shining all-women's world of Artemis, they are unexpectedly drawn to each other. This engaging first book in the trilogy has it all—romance, mystery, and adventure.
A Lambda Literary Award Finalist $9.99

ISIS RISING
Jean Stewart
In this stirring romantic fantasy, the familiar cast of lovable characters begin to rebuild the colony of Isis, burned to the ground ten years earlier by the dread Regulators. But evil forces threaten to destroy their dream. A swashbuckling futuristic adventure and an endearing love story all rolled into one. $11.99

WARRIORS OF ISIS
Jean Stewart
At last, the third lusty tale of high adventure and passionate romance among the Freeland Warriors. Arinna Sojourner, the evil product of genetic engineering, vows to destroy the fledgling colony of Isis with her incredible psychic powers. Whit, Kali, and other warriors battle to save their world, in this novel bursting with life, love, heroines and villains.
A Lambda Literary Award Finalist $11.99

EMERALD CITY BLUES
Jean Stewart
When the comfortable yuppie world of Chris Olson and Jennifer Hart collides with the desperate lives of Reb and Flynn, two lesbian runaways struggling to survive on the streets of Seattle, the forecast is trouble. A gritty, enormously readable novel of contemporary lesbigay life which raises real questions about the meaning of family and community, and about the walls we construct. A celebration of the healing powers of love. $11.99

ROUGH JUSTICE
Claire Youmans
When Glenn Lowry's sunken fishing boat turns up four years after his disappearance, foul play is suspected. Classy, ambitious Prosecutor Janet Schilling immediately launches a murder investigation which produces several surprising suspects—one of them her own former lover Catherine Adams, now living a reclusive life on an island. A real page-turner! $10.99

AND LOVE CAME CALLING
Beverly Shearer
A timeless story of love between two women whose lives are worlds apart—of passion, danger and revenge during the rough and ready days of the Old West. $11.99 [Avail. 9/98]

CORNERS OF THE HEART
Leslie Grey

A captivating novel of love and suspense in which beautiful French-born Chris Benet and English professor Katya Michaels meet and fall in love. But their budding love is shadowed by a vicious killer, whom they must outwit. Your heart will pound as the story races to its heart-stopping conclusion. $9.95

DANGER IN HIGH PLACES
Sharon Gilligan

Set against the backdrop of Washington, D.C., this riveting mystery introduces freelance photographer and amateur sleuth, Alix Nicholson. Alix stumbles on a deadly scheme, and with the help of a lesbian congressional aide, unravels the mystery. $9.99

DANGER! CROSS CURRENTS
Sharon Gilligan

The exciting sequel to *Danger in High Places* brings freelance photographer Alix Nicholson face-to-face with an old love and a murder. When Alix's landlady turns up dead, and her much younger lover, Leah Claire, is the prime suspect, Alix launches a frantic campaign to find the real killer. $9.99

PLAYING FOR KEEPS
Stevie Rios

In this sparkling tale of love and adventure, Lindsay West, a musician, travels to Caracas, where she meets three people who change her life forever: Rob Heron a gay man, who becomes her dearest friend; Her lover Mercedes Luego, who takes Lindsay on a life-altering adventure down the Amazon River; And the mysterious jungle-dwelling woman Arminta, who touches their souls. $10.99

NIGHTSHADE
Karen Williams

Alex Spherris finds herself the new owner of a magical bell, which some people would kill for. With this bell, she is ushered into a strange & wonderful world and meets Orielle, who melts her frozen heart. A heartwarming romance spun in the best tradition of storytelling. $11.99

DREAMCATCHER
Lori Byrd

This timeless story of love and friendship introduces Sunny Calhoun, a college student, who falls in love with Eve Phillips, a literary agent. A richly woven novel capturing the wonder and pain of love between a younger and an older woman. $9.99

AGENDA FOR MURDER
Joan Albarella

Though haunted by memories of love and loss from her years of service in Viet Nam, Nikki Barnes is finally putting back the pieces of her life, and learning to feel again. But she quickly realizes that the college where she teaches is no haven from violence and death, as she comes face to face with murder and betrayal in this least likely of all places—her college campus. $11.99 [Avail. 9/98]

HEARTSTONE AND SABER
Jacqui Singleton
You can almost hear the sabers clash in this rousing tale of good and evil, of passionate love between a bold warrior queen and a beautiful healer with magical powers. $10.99

SHADOWS AFTER DARK
Ouida Crozier
Fans of vampire erotica will adore this! When wings of death spread over Kyril's home world, she is sent to Earth on a mission—find a cure for the deadly disease. Once here, she meets and falls in love with Kathryn, who is enthralled yet horrified to learn that her mysterious, darkly exotic lover is...a vampire. This tender, beautifully written love story is the ultimate lesbian vampire novel! $9.95

FEATHERING YOUR NEST: An Interactive Workbook & Guide to a Loving Lesbian Relationship
Gwen Leonhard, M.ED./Jennie Mast, MSW
This fresh, insightful guide and workbook for lesbian couples provides effective ways to build and nourish your relationships. Includes fun exercises & creative ways to spark romance, solve conflict, fight fair, conquer boredom, spice up your sex lives & enjoy life together. Plus much more. $14.99

TROPICAL STORM
Linda Kay Silva
Another winning, action-packed adventure/romance featuring smart and sassy heroines, an exotic jungle setting, and a plot with more twists and turns than a coiled cobra. Megan has disappeared into the Costa Rican rain forest and it's up to Delta and Connie to find her. Can they reach Megan before it's too late? Will Storm risk everything to save the woman she loves? Fast-paced, full of wonderful characters and surprises. Not to be missed. $11.99

SWEET BITTER LOVE
Rita Schiano
Susan Fredrickson is a woman of fire and ice—a successful high-powered executive, she is by turns sexy and aloof. And from the moment writer Jenny Ceretti spots her at the Village Coffeehouse, her serene life begins to change. As their friendship explodes into a blazing love affair, Jenny discovers that all is not as it appears, while Susan is haunted by ghosts from a her past. Schiano serves up passion and drama in this roller-coaster romance. $10.99

SIDE DISH
Kim Taylor
She's funny, she's attractive, she's lovable—and she doesn't know it. Meet Muriel, aka Mutt, a twenty-something wayward waitress with a college degree, who has resigned herself to low standards, simple pleasures, and erotic fantasies. Though seeming to get by on margaritas and old movies, in her heart of hearts, Mutt is actually searching for true love. While Mutt chases the bars with her best friend, Jeff, she is, in turn, chased by Diane, a former college classmate with a decidedly romantic agenda. When a rich bitch Beverly Hills lawyer named Allison steals Mutt's heart, she is in for trouble, and like the glamorous facade of Sunset Boulevard, things are not quite as they seem.

Teetering on the edge, Mutt survives shattered crushes, harassment from a punked-out chick, and lousy tips. Along the way, she learns a little of what love is really about. $11.99

NO WITNESSES
Nancy Sanra
This cliff-hanger of a mystery set in San Francisco, introduces Detective Tally McGinnis, whose ex-lover Pamela Tresdale is arrested for the grisly murder of a wealthy Texas heiress. Tally rushes to the rescue despite friends' warnings, and is drawn once again into Pamela's web of deception and betrayal as she attempts to clear her and find the real killer. $9.99

NO ESCAPE
Nancy Sanra
This edgy, fast-paced sequel to *No Witnesses*, also set in picturesque San Francisco, is a story of drugs, love and jealousy. Late one rain-drenched night, nurse Melinda Morgan is found murdered. Who cut her life short, plunging a scalpel into her heart, then disappeared into the night? As lesbian PI Tally McGinnis sorts through the bizarre evidence, she can almost sense the diabolical Marsha Cox lurking in the shadows. You will be shocked by the secrets behind the grisly murder. $11.99

DEADLY RENDEZVOUS
Diane Davidson
A string of brutal murders in the middle of the desert plunges Lieutenant Toni Underwood and her lover Megan into a high profile investigation which uncovers a world of drugs, corruption and murder, as well as the dark side of the human mind. An explosive, fast-paced, action-packed whodunit. $9.99

DEADLY GAMBLE
Diane Davidson
Former police detective Toni Underwood is catapulted back into the world of crime by a mysterious letter from her favorite aunt. Black sheep of the family and a prominent madam, Vera Valentine fears she is about to be murdered—a distinct possibility, given her underworld connections. With the help of onetime partner (and possibly future lover) Sergeant Sally Murphy, Toni takes on the seamy, ruthless underbelly of Las Vegas, where appearance and reality are often at odds. Flamboyant characters and unsavory thugs make for a cast of likely suspects... and keep the reader guessing until the last page. $11.99

CLOUD NINE AFFAIR
Katherine E. Kreuter
Chris Grandy—rebellious, wealthy, twenty-something—has disappeared in India, along with her hippie lover Monica Ward. Desperate to bring her home, Christine's millionaire father hires expert Paige Taylor. But the trail to Christine is mined with obstacles, as powerful enemies plot to eliminate her. A witty, sophisticated & entertaining mystery. $11.99

COMING ATTRACTIONS
Bobbi D. Marolt
It's been three years since she's made love to a woman; three years that she's buried herself in work as a successful columnist for one of New York's top newspapers. Helen Townsend admits, at last, she's tired of being lonely....and of being closeted. Enter Princess Charming in the shapely form of Cory Chamberlain, a gifted concert pianist. And Helen embraces joy once again. But can two lovers find happiness when one yearns to break out of the closet and breathe free, while the other fears that will destroy her career? A sunny blend of humor & heart, politics & passion. A novel which captures the bliss and blunderings of love. $11.99

HOW TO ORDER

TITLE   **AUTHOR**   **PRICE**

❑ Agenda for Murder-Joan Albarella 11.99
❑ And Love Came Calling-Beverly Shearer 11.99
❑ Cloud 9 Affair-Katherine Kreuter 11.99
❑ Coming Attractions-Bobbi Marolt 11.99
❑ Corners of the Heart-Leslie Grey 9.95
❑ Danger! Cross Currents-Sharon Gilligan 9.99
❑ Danger in High Places-Sharon Gilligan 9.95
❑ Deadly Gamble-Diane Davidson 11.99
❑ Deadly Rendezvous-Diane Davidson 9.99
❑ Dreamcatcher-Lori Byrd 9.99
❑ Emerald City Blues-Jean Stewart 11.99
❑ Feathering Your Nest-Gwen Leonhard/ Jennie Mast 14.99
❑ Heartstone and Saber-Jacqui Singleton 10.99
❑ Isis Rising-Jean Stewart 11.99
❑ Nightshade-Karen Williams 11.99
❑ No Escape-Nancy Sanra 11.99
❑ No Witnesses-Nancy Sanra 9.99
❑ Playing for Keeps-Stevie Rios 10.99
❑ Return to Isis-Jean Stewart 9.99
❑ Rough Justice-Claire Youmans 10.99
❑ Shadows After Dark-Ouida Crozier 9.99
❑ Side Dish-Kim Taylor 11.99
❑ Sweet Bitter Love-Rita Schiano 10.99
❑ Tropical Storm-Linda Kay Silva 11.99
❑ Warriors of Isis-Jean Stewart 11.99

Please send me the books I have checked. I enclose a check or money order (not cash), plus $3 for the first book and $1 for each additional book to cover shipping and handling. Or bill my ❑Visa/Mastercard ❑Amer. Express.
Or call our Toll Free Number 1-800-648-5333 if using a credit card.
CARD # _____ EXP.DATE_____

SIGNATURE_____

NAME (PLEASE PRINT) _____

ADDRESS _____

CITY_____ STATE_____ ZIP_____
❑ Arizona residents add 7% tax to total.
    RISING TIDE PRESS, 3831 N. ORACLE RD., TUCSON AZ 85705